Song Dogs

A Rory Daggett Story

Praise for the Buzzard's Edge Saga

"Brennan LaFaro's dark world of Buzzard's Edge takes the best elements of the weird western genre and spins them into an expanding mythology that rivals those of Stephen King's Castle Rock, H. P. Lovecraft's Arkham, and Brian Keene's Labyrinth. It's just that damn good!"

Ronald Kelly, author of *Fear* and *The Saga of Dead-Eye*

"LaFaro constructs a unique western horror universe, filled with magic, ballad-worthy tales, and pockets of gory horror."

Drew Huff, author of *The Divine Flesh*

"Grabs you by the neck from page one and it's full steam ahead 'til the end of the line."

Brian McAuley, author of *Curse of the Reaper*

"*The Batman* meets *Django Unchained*. LaFaro takes to the West with this story of revenge and blood."

Scott J. Moses, author of *Our Own Unique Affliction*

"Burning with loneliness and small-town insularity, *Noose* is a chilling addition to the western horror genre. A vicious ear-worm that will keep you humming long after you put the book down."

Lee Murray, *USA Today* Bestselling author and 4-time Bram Stoker Award-winner

"Elements of horror and fantasy pop up in this genre-blurring story about family, loyalty, and good versus evil."

Booklist

"Fast-paced and highly entertaining. Brennan LaFaro comes out with both guns blazing!"

Jonathan Maberry, *NY Times* bestselling author of *Cave 13* and *The Sleepers War*

"LaFaro snaps the reins taut and keeps the gallop strong. The characters and events herein are scrawled in dust and sap, framed in rawhide and wire and hung on your heart."

John Boden, feller what wrote *Snarl*

Song Dogs

A Rory Daggett Story

by Brennan LaFaro

Song Dogs

Copyright 2025 © Brennan LaFaro

This book is a work of fiction. All of the characters, organizations, and events portrayed in this story are either products of the author's imagination or are used fictitiously. Any resemblance to actual events or locales or persons, living or dead, is entirely coincidental.

All rights reserved. No part of this publication may be reproduced in any form or by any means without the express written permission of the publisher, except in the case of brief excerpts in critical reviews or articles. Nor can this publication be used in any manner for the purposes of AI data scraping and training.

No AI has been involved in the production of this book.

All opinions expressed by characters in relation to magic and religion are their personal opinions and are subject to the rules of their universe, which are different from the rules of ours. No characters are scholars in this area, and all are simply coming from a place of trying to do good.

Edited by: Candace Nola
Formatted by: Stephanie Ellis
Cover illustration by: Val Halvorson

First Edition: December, 2025

ISBN (paperback): 978-1-963355-35-2
ISBN (ebook): 978-1-963355-34-5
Library of Congress Control Number:

BRIGIDS GATE PRESS
Overland Park, Kansas
www.brigidsgatepress.com
Printed in the United States of America

BOOKS BY BRENNAN LAFARO

Buzzard's Edge

Noose
The Demon of Devil's Cavern
Where the Daybreak Ends
Song Dogs

Slattery Falls

Slattery Falls
Decimated Dreams
The World You Loved
I Will Always Find You

Standalone

Last Stay
Illusions of Isolation: Thirteen Stories
The Denizens

Content Warnings

Blood
Gore
Gun violence
Murder
Violence toward animals
Violence by animals
Animal death
Disfigurement

For Candace,
Pack, family. It all comes to the same.

AUTHOR'S NOTE

If you've made it this far following Rory, Alice, and the rest of the rabble in Buzzard's Edge, then you already know that this version of the Old West contains all the things people feared when they hitched up their wagons and set out toward unexplored territory, as well as a few things they didn't know to fear yet. As such, I've taken liberties with the Arizona geography, creature names, initial discovery of some of the shadowy things herein, and historical accuracy in sacrifice of story.

Saddle up, let's kick up some dust.

Chapter 1

The World at the End of the Saloon

Do you know what a burnt body smells like? I do. Have for a while now. Not burning. Burnt. There's a difference.

It's how I knew that when a blaze ripped through the Saloon at the End of the World and the building wound up reduced to nothing but char and ash, there had still been two people inside.

One way I knew, at least.

From strolling the evening streets of Buzzard's Edge with Alice by my side, to the porcine figure of Mayor Harvey leaning over his balcony at the Scarlet Revolver, bellowing something about a fire, then a mad dash to collect the newly minted Sheriff Thaddeus Locke from his offices. The fire had mostly burned itself out by the time we arrived. Smoke filled the sky, and the saloon was a loss. Of course that was no comfort, nor burden, to the first corpse we found inside.

"Mortimer Everlie," said Locke. His shiny badge caught a trace of moonlight as he crouched down next to a coal-black husk you could barely talk me into thinking used to be a person.

Taking a step back, I swiped a hand across my nose to banish a little of the stink that filled the air. "He owned the joint, sure enough, but how do you know it's him?"

"I don't. Not positively and not yet. The remnants of clothing are that of a man rather than a woman, and the build is akin to the slight Mr. Everlie. A small man with little fat on his person would produce a somewhat less abhorrent aroma than a larger man, and that Everlie's redolence should contain the scent of overcooked meat with a touch less than usual of the pungent sting which often accompanies burning fat, I can deduce there was not much fat for the fire to consume. Not to the point of identification, Rory, but do you notice a hint of sweetness present in the fragrance? That is burnt spinal fluid you smell, and suggests the immolation was … complete."

Crossing my arms, I took a minute to decide whether or not I could hold my sick in after that educational lecture. Turned out I could. "That's all well and good, Thad, but there's a simple way to nail down your theories."

Slowly, he stood to attention and eyed me with a trace of suspicion, waiting for me to spit it out.

"Well, Mort's standing right over there. And he's not alone."

Only a couple months had passed since the Devil's Cavern massacre, and my little trip to the dark frontier before that, the one that left me seeing shadows of the dead around every corner. The talent wasn't as all-consuming as it had been on day one. Not anymore. Still lingered, though. Especially with fresh ghosts. You could always pick them out. Blurry memories of what a human being should look like set in a dim gray.

Locke's eyes softened. "I thought that was fading."

"Fading ain't the same as gone," I said, trying and failing to keep frustration out of my voice.

Locke scanned the wreckage of the Saloon at the End of the World. Charred stools, a blackened rib cage that used to be a piano, glittering pebbles of burst glass, and floorboards curled up from the heat. No other bodies at first glance.

"Who is it?" he asked. "The other one."

"Jules, I think her name was." I gave it a second to see if the young woman might nod a confirmation. She just kept staring straight ahead. "Can't say I came in here all that often, but I do believe she ran the place when Mort wasn't around."

"May I ask what they're doing?"

Standing perfectly still, unnatural still, staring right fucking at me, and their mouths are moving like they've got something so goddamn important to tell me. Except I can't hear a sound. Like there's a world between us and it murks the sights and kills the sounds. Mort with his beady little rodent eyes, a shine of regret in the dark of his pupils. The woman, taller by half a head, and she looks so scared, with sad, empty eyes. Then they drifted away like they're made of Sonoran sand and a breeze took 'em.

"Nothing," I said. "They're gone."

Locke nodded, and I wondered if he believed me. "The pattern of the glass," he said. "Do you notice anything?"

Smartassery evaded me for the moment, and I shook my head.

"It's too all-encompassing for my liking," he said. "The heat would burst the bottles stowed behind the counter, of course, and the odd bit might find its way far from the original location. Not quite in the surplus that exists beneath the piano, say, or by the doorway."

I followed his outstretched finger, and though I might not have picked it up on my best day, there was something to what Locke said. Too much glass collected in too concentrated an area for the laws of chaos.

"You think someone set it on purpose?" I asked.

"I think the scene certainly points an accusatory finger. To learn there should be a second body, and away from the vicinity of the first? Surely if the fire had erupted suddenly, the other person could escape easily enough by running out the front door." He met my eyes and softened his voice. "Unless both were killed before the fire was set. I make my bones by allowing coincidence only so much rope to hang itself."

As if on cue, something creaked from behind the bar. No. Farther back.

"Back room," I said. "What's left of it, anyway."

Locke squinted in that direction. "A moment, if you please. I'd like to check one more thing here." Crouching down, he began to prod at the overdone corpse of Mort Everlie.

"Catch up when you can."

"Be careful, my friend." His eyes never left the body when he said it, but there was care in those words. I guess we'd come a long way.

As I made to turn, Locke spoke once more, stopping me in my tracks like he'd grabbed my shoulder with an invisible hand. "What about the girl?"

Alice. For some reason, he refused to call her anything but "the girl."

"Outside and armed," I said, the whisper of a question mark hovering around the end of it.

Locke shook his head. "I only meant is her newfound talent faded or gone?"

"A damn good question. I hope to be able to answer it truthfully someday soon."

Truth is, I saw the dead after they died. Alice saw them before.

Just a nod from Thad. It was as good as a quick squeeze on the shoulder.

Creeping toward the back room, I pulled my revolver, the very one that belonged to my adoptive father, Henry Taff, and which had served me well for a few years now. Bullets wouldn't do much against the sputtered-out flames. The building's crispy skeleton could be settling still, but guilty footsteps putting their weight on flame-weak floorboards seemed more likely. As Locke had said, coincidence just ran out of rope.

I threw open the door and let the barrel of my revolver peek inside. I knew this little backroom far more intimately than I'd ever known the main gathering area of the saloon. It was where I'd hallucinated a phantom train ride, listened to my parents' killer blow his own brains out, and eventually come to some kind of odd truce with his spirit.

George "Noose" Holcomb.

Whatever was left of the man's ghost was long gone from the saloon's storage space. Moonlight stared down holes the fire had eaten through the roof. It wasn't enough to grant me a clear view. I stepped inside, testing my weight on a soft patch of wood, then tried again until I found firm purchase. Inside, the vague outline of a deserted room and the first warning of movement.

"Shit." Not loud enough to draw Locke's attention.

Something roughly the size and shape of a cougar, sleek and low to the ground. Crouched down into a stance like—

Then I heard it. The unmistakable sound of a predator's teeth separating skin from muscle, tendon from bone. A wet tearing followed by loud, slurping gulps.

Jules, I thought, and like it could hear my mind working, the cougar lifted its head to show me it was pretty fucking far from a cougar. Bright red embers glowed in its eyes, trails of fire running from them down the sides of its body and outlining its form. *Bathed in flames.* The words raced through my mind as I tried to make heads or tails of this thing. Two pointed horns rose from its brow, giving it a look like some unholy cross between a mountain lion and a pronghorn with a head full of fire.

Fuck the horns, I thought. *Buzzard's Edge ain't never seen a cougar that big.*

I squeezed the butt of my gun, thinking to put a bullet in its skull. Only it didn't look like the kind of creature that likes to be shot at. Somebody else was welcome to wing it and piss it off. I wasn't the one drawing a sheriff's salary. Slowly, I took a step backward.

"Hey Thad," I whispered.

No answer from the scorched remains of the end of the world.

The monster growled a sound like the earth was about to open up. Hell, with all those burnt-up floorboards, maybe it was. Then it padded forward, a kind of slow saunter that only a beast who knows its advantage can muster. Darkness still hid a fair portion of the cougar's body, even with those traces of fire traveling from its eyes and glowing all around its massive body. Its tail flicked, accompanied by a hiss and a small puff of flame.

"Thad, I think this thing just farted a fireball."

Shoot or run.

Fuck it, why not both?

An intersection on the railroad of thought, I raised my revolver and let it sing.

Bullets dimpled the ember-riddled shadows that made up the monster's body. Rather than retreat, it stood to its full height, and a plume of flame flooded my way. The white-hot fire swirled around its form, giving me the clearest picture yet. A beast that stood as many hands tall as my horse, Ghost, with razor-sharp tips on those horns and inky black fur that explained how it could melt into the shadows so easily.

"Locke," I screamed, and his footsteps pounded against the floor, racing toward me. I rolled away from the freshly ignited wood, almost too rotted to burn any further, and a few things happened that damn near stopped my heart and made me doubt my sanity. The monster unleashed another deluge of flame, straight from its fucking gullet, I shit you not, and I just barely rolled out of the way a second time. Then it turned and coiled on its haunches, revealing an odd tail, dark green and scaled and … bear with me, complete with a nasty little fanged head at the end. Like somebody nailed a Mojave green to the cougar-thing's ass. No sooner had I come to terms with this oddity than a pair of wings sprouted from its back, dark and scaly to match that obscene tail. The wings blocked out the moonlight, then flapped with a great whoosh of air and carried the creature up through the crumbling remains of the roof and into the night sky.

The whole encounter seemed to last forever, yet the creature was a speck against the moon when Locke burst into the room and found me lying in a pile of ash with one sleeve still smoking.

"I'll be fucked," I said to the mild look of consternation spread across his face.

As always with Locke, he surveyed the room in a flash, his cunning eyes cutting from place to place and cataloguing everything he saw with ruthless efficiency. He stopped when his eyes landed on Jules's body. Shock and horror made a show in his eyes before he buried both, replacing them with a flat deadpan.

"What happened?" he asked.

"Not sure you'd believe me if I told you. Not sure I believe it myself. But if it's all the same, I think I'd rather tell you later. Suddenly doesn't feel so safe here."

Locke resumed his search and let a few seconds tick off his internal clock, then simply said, "Alright."

He helped me to my feet and started toward the open area of the saloon when a whining creak came from behind us. Like spurs scratching glass, it sent a wave of nerves up my spine. From our left, where I knew there to be a closet, the wall collapsed inward, belching a puff of smoke and tackling us to the ground. Though the blaze was mostly extinguished by the time we had arrived, an ember had evidently survived behind the wall and lay in wait to stop us leaving. A corroded beam pinned me to the floor at the knee and Locke's pained grunts told me he found himself in a similar predicament.

Each on our high lonely, we fought the weight of the former building off ourselves and crawled low toward freedom. Just shy of the threshold, I placed a hand and, a bit too late, remembered the spongy flooring I'd squished on the way in. Beneath me, the floor broke away and I plunged through.

Sand. It should have been nothing but fucking sand. Instead, it was deeper than a desert grave by a fair pinch. My misplaced weight carried me forward, fast enough to miss any handholds, slow enough to spot the gleaming, jagged metal pieces strewn about the bottom. The deadly items raced closer, then came to a sudden stop when a hand latched onto my ankle.

Thad Locke. Lord bless and keep that man.

He held me suspended for a moment, sweat dripping off the end of my nose to fall and collect on an upturned spade right beside a serrated knife with its hilt buried in the ground, a host of strategically placed carpenter's nails, and a variety of other hazards I couldn't put a name to before he yanked me out of that hole and wrestled me back into the saloon.

"You saved me," I said, dumbly, sitting back on my haunches.

"A trap." An uncharacteristic fear settled in his eyes as a series of bruises bloomed along his cheeks.

"What makes you think that?"

It was a stupid question, and he chastised me with a look that said as much.

"No sub-basement, that. And it makes me wonder if the wall's collapse was a true accident." He bit his lip, then went on. "Also, Rory, does it seem to you a strange coincidence that this building should be burned to the ground under odd circumstances when Mr. Meyer's wood shop met the same fate only two weeks ago?"

"I hadn't thought of it." I blew out a deep sigh. "Well, freedom first. Suspicion, later. God forbid that fire took out another damn wall and just let us out of here." I pointed to his legs. "How's your lower half holding up?"

Locke smiled with a cruelty I'd seen before, one that made me glad he was on my side. "It will be stiff and sore tomorrow, but it won't betray me today."

"Likewise. So, any reason we can't presume it's safe to sit here all day?"

"Besides the fire kindling inside the wall?"

"Yeah," I said. "Besides that."

"If pressed, I suppose I'd say because your young ward is outside unaccompanied."

"She's armed."

"Indeed. And presumably, she heard the sound of gunshots a moment ago and has yet to make an appearance."

Cold like a desert night settled in my stomach. The man was right. At the very least, Alice should have been poking her head through the door to make sure everything was alright. "Your magic eyes see anything obvious that's going to trip us up or eat us alive?"

"Nothing sticks out, but—"

With a slap on my knees, I sprang up and stuck out a foot, feeling for any more soft spots on the boards. They creaked and complained as Locke stood to join me, and slowly, eyes peeled, we made our way across the open room. It stretched on for goddamn miles. A space that stood packed to the walls with people on any other night suddenly seemed large enough to house the entire town and part of Dusty Springs, as well. We took every step with care because who knew what might be at the bottom of the next pit?

We'd made it about five feet when the first gunshot came.

It zipped in through one of the windows and kicked up a mix of splinters and ash. An earsplitting crack, and a second slug dug in just behind my feet.

"A rifle, then," said Locke, as he ducked down and pressed himself against the bar. Soot fell from the countertop, settling on his shoulders. "Stay together. Keep low. Hands and knees. Present a minimal target. Move with care and haste."

"Your levelheadedness is equal parts refreshing and maddening."

Locke may or may not have heard me. He was off and I was already breaking the first rule. In recompense, I squeezed low and chased his ass, trying to distribute my weight as evenly as possible as the shots started up again, zipping through fire-eaten holes in the wall and scraping up the floorboards in their search for fleshier targets.

A crack, a squelch, and a muffled grunt, and I knew one of the bullets had found an unwelcome home in old Thad. Still, he kept up the pace, and I scuttled along behind him, waiting for my turn. It wasn't long before one of the stray shots bit into my calf just above the boot, taking a scrap of flesh with it, and sending a spray of blood heavenward.

Could've been worse, but that line of thought hardly made me embrace it.

"Shouldn't we be firing back?" I grumbled as we took temporary shelter beneath the skeleton of the piano.

"A rifle, as I said. Presumably with an enviable line of sight and the advantage of high ground. The two direct hits suggest they can see our movements in part, but perhaps not clearly. Firing back would only fill in the missing pieces of the picture."

"Got it. Scurry like rodents and pray to the almighty for a shade of invisibility."

"Exactly that. Come, Daggett. A few more feet to the door and once we break cover, we should be able to discover the location of the shooter."

"You don't think—"

Another shot rang out, ripping the words straight from off my tongue.

Locke's eyes went wide to match my own. I think he knew the sound of that second gun, and I sure as hell did.

"That's Alice, and she's laying down cover. Shit on a Sunday, Thad, let's fuckin' move!"

We dashed for the door, no more thoughts for dagger-lined graves and hidden hearth fires. One hand holding my hat down, I burst into the moonlight, raised my revolver high and searched the rooftops for any glint of a rifle or murderous silhouettes. Nothing. No reflection, no crunch of boots on rooftop dust, no scrape of heels making a clean getaway, and certainly not the high-powered click of the last rifle shot I'd ever hear.

Nothing but my own heavy breathing and Mr. Locke's next to me. Winded from the exertion and simultaneously relieved we'd escaped our intended tomb.

A trap, he'd said, and the word rang true. The only mystery was who set it.

But the fire had only started a couple hours ago, and hadn't it burned itself out quickly? Certainly seemed the work of more than one man and—

The monster. The fucking monster. You think one guy corralled that goddamn thing into the back room all by his lonesome?

"Mr. Daggett, Mr. Locke." The voice was booming, almost boisterous, and I knew it. Just not right away, not under the circumstances. Faster than a dust devil, I spun toward the sound and aimed my revolver between a lively set of eyes. Truth be told, I barely recognized them from street level.

Bigger than life and pushing against the constraints of a pair of tweed pants and a matching jacket was Mayor Moses Harvey. He stood sideways to us, like we'd caught him passing by, and he stopped to tip his hat. A broad grin swept across his face, peeking out from under a thick, black mustache. A little relief coursed through my veins at the sight of him.

Until he turned and revealed a gun in his hand, pressed into Alice's white-blonde hair.

CHAPTER 2

STARS IN HER EYES

Moses Harvey had two guns aimed at his giant head and appeared as worried about it as a preacher on Sunday evening after his sermon was packed away.

"What's this about?" asked Locke.

You had to admire him, balls hefty enough to threaten the life of the man who paid his salary.

With Harvey's attention engaged, I turned my free hand palm up and flicked it back and forth before turning it over with pointer and middle finger outstretched. Quick as a flash, but Alice's eyes told me she caught the sign.

What happened?

"Ah no, I don't think so, Daggett," said Harvey. "None of this secretive shit between you and the kid. You want to talk, let's do it in a way everyone can understand."

"Fair enough. Can we start with what the fuck, Mr. Mayor? Or Thad's polite version if you like … What the fuck is this about and why do you have a gun pointed at my little girl?"

Moses's eyes wandered the streets, and I followed, looking for a reemergence of the shooter. Alice's one shot. It hadn't taken out Harvey, and the girl didn't miss. If there was a second shooter, she must've hit him or scared him off. Still no sign, then I had a realization. "You don't want anybody to see us out here. Dead of night, and I bet you hoped drawing us to that booby-trapped building would prove enough."

"Alas, here we stand," added Locke.

"Alas, indeed," I said.

Harvey looked uncomfortable for a hair, then hid it behind a grin and dug the gun barrel deeper into the side of Alice's head. With the size of the man's hands, I hadn't realized at first the pistol was near big enough to fire chicken eggs. Alice grimaced and pulled away, flashed me some kind of look I couldn't decode, then made an L with her thumb, pointer and middle, giving the latter two fingers a wag.

Not bad, Pip. Not bad.

Eyes continuing to roam, Harvey appeared blissfully unaware of our silent conversation as long as it came from Alice's end. "There was a fire a couple weeks back, gentlemen. Took Mr. Meyer's building clear to the ground. Or did you forget?"

Walking back from Devil's Cavern seemed half a lifetime ago. Come to think of it, I guess I'd seen Harvey waddle along that day as well. He'd been far away from us when we unpacked what had happened. On top of Ghost, Alice had raised her hands, flat palms facing inward, and moved the right in front of the left. *Next.* A little give and take and we'd come to understand her plunge in Mary Crane's resurrection pool left her with the ability to see things yet to come.

Her face paled, eyes distant, and for a moment she was gone. Scary gone.

"Pip," I whispered and gave her a good shake.

Eyes closer to focused, she gave me a dull smile and closed her right fist, then slid it along a flat left palm. *Woodwork.* Meyer's shop. Easy enough, at least after we'd exhausted some possibilities. Two hands, fingers wriggling, passing up, down, and around, like she was juggling. *Fire.* Two closed fists, moving together in a circle. Once, twice. Then her hands sprung open, palms down. That one I had to ask for again before my brain caught up.

Magic.

What the hell does that mean? When? Why? What the hell? Those questions and dozens more escaped my lips as we rode home. Alice just shook her head.

There'd been only one occurrence, and every day I waited for her to get the same far-eyed look she'd come down with when I asked her to tell me everything. It was like she'd had a flash of momentary inspiration, and once the wick burned through, it was all gone. For a time, anyway.

"Man lost his life in that fire," continued Harvey. "My brother. And from what I've gathered, there were only four others present at the moment Jack Harvey sucked in his last breath. The three of you and Mr. Everlie in there. Because you didn't have the decency to die like dogs in the saloon, I guess I have to do it myself. Before I do, and to bandy from your own vernacular, care to tell me what the fuck that night at Meyer's was all about? Some folk saw yous milling around the time the fire broke out, so don't try any good Samaritan shit."

I passed a look with Locke. His voice and expression evidently had an agreement to say nothing.

"Truth's kind of hard to swallow," I said.

"I've got a big appetite."

"Jesus, okay. That girl, there," I said. "The one small enough to be up past her bedtime, the one you're an inch away from rupturing her eardrum with a gun barrel. That girl? She saw it before it happened. The outline, the shape. A general idea. No idea what it meant. Then poof. Gone! Like it was some fluke thing. Then, Mr. Harvey, the afternoon of the fire, she broke into a cold sweat. Skin pale, eyes wide, and she kept signing the same thing. 'Tonight.' Over and over. Took half the damn afternoon to figure out what she meant. By the time we got there, it was too late. Fire started just about the time we walked in the door."

I wet my lips against the night, neglecting the part of the story where our appearance may have caused the fire.

"There were two men in there, bandanas covering both their faces," I said. "One about your size, the other kind of scrawny. You tell me it was your brother and Mort Everlie, that makes sense. I didn't know it at the time, though. Neither did Alice nor Thad. Swear that to you. Now, would you mind moving that gun away from Alice?"

He ignored my request. "That's all very convenient and sounds about as full of horseshit as the Aegean stables. Any word from you, Mr. Locke?"

Before Thad could continue his stony silence, Alice shot me a look that said, "Stop flapping your lips and just do like I asked."

I obliged. Fingers on my free hand up and in my mouth before Harvey could register anything wrong, and I let out a piercing whistle. Alice tore herself free and hit the sand before Harvey could calculate the sudden change in situation.

Hooves thundered against the ground as Ghost burst from an alley, a flash of black and white blurred to gray, enough to put the remaining drifts of smoke trailing off the saloon to shame. She closed the gap to Mayor Harvey in half a heartbeat and reared up to add a few new dents to his head.

Stepping back, I watched the mayor's eyes for any trace of fear and found none. His hand snapped up like a trained military man and a puff of smoke accompanied a great boom. All I could do was stand and stare as a hole opened up under Ghost's chin and a tuft of her mane blew back, shooting a mix of brain and bone up toward the moon.

Alice unleashed a cry as I'd only heard her make once or twice before. A quick, guttural sob that bypassed the voice box on its way straight from the soul. When Ghost's forelegs clattered to the ground, and she stood there swaying for a moment, I prayed I'd misjudged the bullet. Invented the image of soaring brain matter. The horse's eyes told me otherwise. They twinkled like they were full of stars, then began to search desperately for me, for Alice, so wide I could see my horrified reflection in them for a split second before she collapsed to the dirt in a heap.

The world stopped spinning, and as much as I'd wish later that I'd wrapped my hands around Mayor Harvey's neck, I'm not sure my legs could've moved if they had wheels. Alice, either. She threw herself on Ghost and buried her face in the horse's mane. Silent sobs racked her small body.

"Nasty trick," said Harvey. "And one you won't be—"

He almost finished the sentence, almost, before the bulk of his right cheek tore away at the behest of Thad Locke's bullet. Had it been a caliber like Harvey's gun, there would have been nothing but a stump geysering where his fucking head used to be. I can't say I would've hated that.

Moses Harvey squealed like a pig in heat, clutching his face as crimson poured between his fingers. He dropped to his knees and his gun crunched to the sand; the sound mostly covered by his screams. That's when I first noticed the faces. Pale, frightened visages poking out of every alley, peering out every window, staring out from the front porches of businesses and homes alike.

How long had Buzzard's Edge been watching?

Long enough to see what he did to Ghost? Long enough to hear the mayor confess to the attempted murder of a town sheriff and a child?

The whispers.

Is that Mayor Harvey?

Too damn big to be anyone else.

Why'd he have a gun pointed at that kid?

He killed that horse. I saw it.

The watchful stares beat down like sunbeams and the Mayor stifled his screams and started to sweat. Might be creatures of the night, judgmental humans, or something more ancient and terrifying altogether, but in Buzzard's Edge, you're always being watched. Count on it.

"You're surrounded, Moses." Locke said it softly. "Best to come quietly."

Harvey's animal eye, the one not shielded by his hand trying to hold the gore in, flew madly around, person to person, building to building, like any one of them could offer a helping hand. Then he nodded, planting an arm in the sand to lift his great bulk.

A tiny squeak came from behind me. Alice, still wrapped in an embrace with Ghost, brought her hands together. One in a fist, the other open and circling to draw attention to the—

Fist.

As soon as the realization hit me, Harvey tossed a fistful of sand into Locke's eyes and made a break twice as quick as a man that large has any right to. Thad brushed at his face, trying to clear his vision, and I started forward before another rifle crack from the rooftops kicked up an explosion of sand between me and Harvey, telling me to stay put.

A second shooter, after all. Alice had quieted him but hadn't managed to put him down.

Tears still in her eyes, Alice grabbed her gun and let off a volley of shots in the general direction of the shooter. Five bangs into the night and no response.

Hands clenched, body coiled, I fought the urge to go after him and risk having my skull dashed to bits alongside Ghost. Alice had already lost one friend today—and would she ever forgive me for that? Didn't seem wholly necessary to put myself at risk chasing down a man the size of a grizzly bear who'd turned the entire town against himself in the blink of an eye.

"Let him go," said Locke, wiping the last grains of sand from his eyes. "He'll either bleed out in a ditch, head west and never return, or the people will bring him to frontier justice." He blinked a few times, then scanned the rooftops. "Just the one shot. I suspect his accomplice has gone to ground as well."

"If they saw what I saw, they probably pissed their pants over a little girl and ran."

Locke nodded, keeping his eyes upward. "Will you help me clear the rooftops? Just to be safe?"

The whispers from all around had diminished to something lesser. Memories, suggestions of conversation past. The vigilant eyes of the town retreated now that there was nothing left to see. Except a slim nine-year-old girl, revolver tossed to the side in the burning sand. Her blue eyes hidden against the cooling fur of a creature who shared her stubborn streak and loved her unconditionally.

The horse's eyes were still filled with stars, only reflections this time.

Around the empty streets, I searched, curious to know if I could see the recently departed spirits of animals as well. No such luck. A strange thought flitted through my head. Maybe I could only see the spirits of those who had died lonely.

"No, Thad," I said. "I think I'd better beg off this once."

Chapter 3

A Few Last Words

Paul Barron, apothecary extraordinaire, lent us the use of his wagon to bring Ghost home, plus an extra pair of shoulders to hoist the old girl onto the wagon bed. The strongest shoulders around since the unexpected disappearance of Mr. Meyer. Paul then offered his horse to take us all back to the homestead. His final overture was a helping hand to dig a queen-sized grave. Alice waved him off without a consult, and truth be told, if she hadn't, I would have done so.

There are some things you're just supposed to do yourself.

The way he nodded told me Paul understood, so he sent us on our way with glistening eyes and well wishes, asking only that we return his property as soon as we finished our business.

We took the trip in silence, then commenced digging in the same manner. My leg stung something fierce from the rifle shot, but there'd be time to clean that up later.

"You're awful quiet," I said, wiping the first drops of sweat from my brow. I forced a smirk my heart didn't quite agree with and waited for one of Alice's fierce scowls. The kind that made sure I knew I wasn't as funny as I thought. The kind I loved. Instead, she just plunged her shovel into the dirt and pried up another hunk.

It wasn't the first body we'd buried together. She was a little taller these days, a lot stronger than the emaciated child I found in the upstairs of my parents' house. Not much more than a skeleton half-starved to death. Now, she had meat on her bones, and she used every last bit of it to open up the earth out in back of our stables to bury her friend. *Our* friend.

"I'm sorry," I said. "I shouldn't've—"

She stopped me with a raised hand. No sign language, that. Just plain old common sense. Alice's way of stating the obvious.

"I told you to call Ghost, and we both know it," that hand said.

Then she started digging again. A ways to go and the sun was only just up.

Silently, I joined in, deciding that my shovel was more use to the moment than my mouth. The ominous chitter of an early-rising cactus wren and the occasionally stamped hoof of Barron's mare, waiting impatiently to be returned, distracted us from the *clink-clank* of the shovels and gave us an excuse to avoid conversing any further.

Hours passed, and finally the hole rose up nearly to my shoulders.

"Time to put the old girl to rest, I reckon."

Alice leaned against her shovel but gave no other sign of affirmation. I understood that. To say "yes" or even nod your head was to give permission to finality. To death.

"I've got this, Pip. You've done enough."

I closed my eyes and lowered my head. Just for a moment. When I opened my eyes, she was gone. Close, but out of sight. Since we'd started work on the house damn near a year before, she'd had a penchant for searching out the shadows and hiding spots. In the town proper, you could never do much of anything without being watched. Out at our ranch, she made it doubly true.

Having Ghost's body wrapped in a canvas tarpaulin made the next task easier, but hardly easy. Thankfully, Barron had sent along a strong and cooperative specimen who took direction from a man she didn't know and helped to gently pull Ghost off the wagon and into the hole. I led her with caution and realized after the fact that I should've arranged all this before we dug. Never buried a horse before, and I didn't particularly want to bury two if Barron's mare took a bad step.

The process was long and exhausting, sweaty. The sun beat down, pulling behind Apollo's chariot, finding itself directly overhead by the time I eased Ghost into her final resting place. I wrapped her in the tarpaulin and made a mental note to replace it or force a few dollars on Paul when he tried to turn them down. Then I picked up the shovel and squeezed the handle, letting the splinters dig into my bare hands. It wasn't that I was afraid of a little more sun and a little more work. Just that I felt like I should say something, if not for my sake, then for Alice's.

All the wrong words spun around in my head. Thankfully, a voice interrupted before I could let any of them loose.

"Awfully warm out here, Mr. Daggett. Thought I might bring you and your girl some sarsaparilla."

It startled me to the point I almost dropped the shovel, then quickly recovered my wits and turned with a nervous smile. The few visitors we got to the ranch were usually either law or outlaw. The woman who smiled back at me didn't appear to be either one.

"That's mighty kind of you, Miss ..."

"Kane," she said, and dropped her gaze in a way that reminded me I was bare from the waist up. The way her long, dark hair fell down past her shoulders and framed a kind, gently lined face with soft brown eyes, I guess didn't mind all that much. A white line of scar traced the edge of her nose on one side, so light you might miss it if you didn't look close. "Hazel Kane. Mr. Locke brought me in to run the schoolhouse when he took up his sheriff duties. The way I understand it, you were tied up in that as well, so I suppose this is as much a thank you for the job, as for unmasking that traitorous—" She peered around like she expected an audience, then dropped her voice to a whisper. "Son of a bitch. The man who ran this town and probably spent most of that goodwill making money hand over fist. Mr. Locke is looking into it, and I expect he'll have some findings pretty soon."

"I expect he will."

Hazel Kane cradled the earth-colored jug of sarsaparilla close to her body while she spied around. "Is your daughter here?"

"Somewhere around here."

Her face drooped. "Oh." I recognized disappointment when I saw it and felt a little pang of it myself.

Desperate to change the subject, I said, "How's things in town? Must be pretty hectic, yeah?"

Her face lit up in a smile, like that was just the question she'd hoped for. "You could certainly say that. One of those situations where a day ago, people generally had positive things to say about Moses Harvey. After last night, it seems everyone's got a story. Half or more are probably nonsense, but from what I can gather about this town, that doesn't matter." Her cheeks went red. "I don't mean to speak ill of your home. My apologies."

"No offense taken. It ain't Eden around here."

She nodded, then caught herself. "Harvey won't be able to show his face in town again. What little Mr. Locke left of it."

"He's a hell of a shot, I guess."

"*Mmhmm*, so those quiet conversations, the ones everybody hears, they're mostly asking the same thing. Who takes the reins from Moses Harvey? I suppose we'll need to have a vote. Only problem is, who's up to the job?"

She raised her eyebrows and let her smile carve into a smirk. When I say I knew what that woman would say before she ever opened her mouth, believe it. "Hey, you could run."

Right on the money.

She continued, "People are never going to have a higher opinion of you than they do at this moment. A smart man would capitalize on that."

"Would he now?"

She held that grin, waiting for me to add another line or two. I'm sorry to say I disappointed her for the second time.

"Well, I guess I just wanted to come on by and say thank you. To both of you. Maybe introduce myself. Can't say I get out this way all that often."

"Probably about as often as I get to the schoolhouse."

"*Hm,*" she said, furrowing her brows. "Which makes me think. Alice—that's her name, right? Alice isn't in school. Perhaps you should consider sending her."

I scratched at the back of my neck. "Guess I hadn't thought of it. She, uh, she can't talk, Miss Kane. Listens just fine, mostly, but uses hand signs to make her needs known. I just don't know how great she'd fare." A kick at the dirt. "I worry."

"American sign language." She shrugged. "I'm not familiar with how to speak it, but I've heard of it. Mr. Daggett, I don't mean to speak out of turn, but a little change of scenery might do Alice well. Not just for her three R's, but to make some friends and experience a world without quite so much … violence." She let the word hang in the air between us. "Think on it, will you? Both things I said."

I nodded and clucked my tongue, not sure whether I'd just been insulted, and if so, how badly. "It was nice to meet you, Miss Kane—"

"Hazel, please."

"Yeah, alright. And you make it Rory. You probably already know we lost our horse last night in the, uh, commotion. Dug her a nice resting place, and we were just preparing to say a few words."

"Of course. Yes. I'll just …" She took a step back and set the jug down. A sweet, almost spicy, smell floated into the air as a splash of dark brown slopped out of the container's mouth and the sand drank it up. She turned around and started back toward town. "Come and visit, like I said, Rory. Don't be a stranger. After all, you're famous now."

Famous? Hopefully, I did a passable job of hiding just how much I hated the sound of that. I gave her a wave, and she kept on toward the horizon.

"I could see myself with a schoolteacher," I muttered as the heat drifting off the sand swirled her form into something unreadable and eventually made it disappear altogether. "Even if she does talk up a storm."

A picture of Mary Crane née McHugh formed in the back of my mind, along with all the shit that had happened the last time a woman showed interest in me.

Turning back toward the grave, there was Alice. She'd snuck up, quiet as ever, and cocked a fist in front of her mouth, index finger fluttering back and forth like she was emptying six bullets from a revolver.

"Well-wisher," I said, and jerked my head toward the jug, heating up under the midday sun. I could've told her Miss Kane's vocation and her suggestions, but that felt like a conversation for another time. "Brought us some libations, anyway. Before we settle inside, I thought I'd say a few words. How about you?"

Alice raised her eyebrows, and for a little minute, the sullen version of that girl took a break. Then she came back, still and thoughtful, before she erupted into a flurry of hand movement. She flattened her right hand and tapped it against her left, then gave a thumbs up and ran it along her jawline. Next, she pointed her index finger like a gun, twirled the entire hand in a circle, and brushed it against her heart. A couple more additions, and even though my mind usually took its sweet time processing, I got every word on the first go. When Alice had said everything she needed to say, her arms slumped by her side, hanging in an exhausted manner, and a single tear slipped down her cheek.

I put my arm around her shoulder and felt her tense. "Couldn't have said it better myself, Pip."

She lifted her hand once more, pointer and pinky up, all her other fingers meeting on her palm, and shook it back and forth a couple times.

I love you and goodbye.

When the standing around was done and it came time to bury the old girl, Alice laid the first shovelful of dirt. Gently, it rained down on Ghost.

CHAPTER 4

PANIC AND A CUP OF TEA

It was three days later when I first heard the name Alexander Farrell. One of those names that sullies your ears from time to time if you spend a good deal of your life frequenting local businesses, particularly houses of dubious repute. To me, it was a new and unexpected set of syllables, followed immediately by a stitched-on bit saying, *Better get to know the man, he's declaring his bid for mayor of Buzzard's Edge.*

Before his name came to grace my ears, the days were quiet. Alice and I spent them attending to matters around the homestead, keeping clear of each other's paths. Maybe not on a conscious level, on my part, at least, but that didn't stop it happening. Once or twice, I made the short trip to town to see if Moses Harvey had stuck his ugly mug out from the shadows. Word was, he'd either died from his wounds or skedaddled off into the desert. It amounted to the same. Point was, the streets were quiet. Mostly.

I'd be lying if I said I hadn't thought of stopping in to say hello to Miss Hazel Kane, even strolled by the schoolhouse more than once, only to find my courage in talking to the fairer sex a mite shy of my ability to face down a murderous mob with nothing but a revolver and a little girl by my side.

I'd get there, eventually. Hazel's smile hadn't left the back of my mind, and neither had her words.

After all, you're famous now.

It had sounded so damn stupid at the time, I wrote off what she'd said and tried to forget it. Almost succeeded too. Until the first watchful Buzzard's Edgian caught sight of me.

"You Rory Daggett?" asked a cockeyed kid, suspicion written all over his face.

"I am."

"My mama says you faced down that bear of a mayor single-handedly. Two guns blazing and refused to back down even when he—"

"Alright, alright," I said, motioning for him to keep his voice down. "I don't remember it being all that dramatic, and I sure had some help, but it's mostly true."

"Guess I thought you'd be taller," said the kid, disappointment leaching into his voice.

"Keeps me from having to duck through doorways. You need somethi—"

"It's him!" screamed the kid. "It's Rory Dagget, the man what gave the mayor what for!"

A dozen heads turned in my direction, judgmental eyes giving way to wide-open surprise. Mouths gaping like they'd never seen a skinny guy wandering through the center of town before. I smiled and waved, feeling myself turn red as an August sunset. Hot as one too.

When the people started to close in, visions of the town descending on our farmhouse to accuse me of murdering Sheriff McHugh buzzed through my head. Not exactly a pleasant memory, but then again, there'd been less smiles that day. Now, it seemed the streets were ripe with them.

A sweaty hand seized my arm and shook it. "Doris Campbell, Mr. Daggett. Can't believe I get to shake your hand."

Somebody with a palm the size of a hornet's nest swatted me on the back. "Proud of ya, son. You did a good thing there. A real good thing. Why that fella Harvey—"

"Say, Daggett. I got a neighbor done shot up my fence posts. Don't s'pose you'd be willing to come on over and settle his hash. I'd be willing to—"

A crusty voice cut through. "Lay off the boy! Lay off him. Now, Daggett, don't listen to the rabble. I've got a genuine opportunity I'd like to discuss with—"

The voices swirled out of time with their faces, like a small cyclone stirred up all the desert sand and swept me up along with it, spinning and prodding at me 'til I couldn't tell what was what.

"Excuse me," I mumbled. "Just trying to get on home." Those little clichés and half a dozen more. Anything that passed through my head that might earn me a little breathing room. The bodies pressed in, friendly as all get out, but hot, sweaty, overwhelming, and most of all loud. "Pardon," I whispered, trying to find a gap in the fleshy mass. "Just trying to get through."

"Drinks on the house anytime, Rory. For you and the girl. Hell, bring her down. We'll make it a show. Way I hear it, she can shoot."

Deep breath. Deep. Deep, deep fucking breath.

Except I couldn't find one. My lungs felt shallower than a puddle.

Eyes closed because I knew if I saw the face of the man who'd just offered to make a show of my Alice, I'd bloody my knuckles right on up.

Deep breath. Deep, deep—

Then I ran. I'm ashamed to say I knocked at least two well-meaning folks back on their asses and perhaps mortally wounded my prospects of running for mayor. One more minute of that madness and I dare say it would've been a can of peaches worse than that. Down the nearest alleyway I dashed, a host of voices calling after me. Some sounded angry or put out, others simply surprised. A stampede of footsteps trailed me, gently suggesting I hop a fence and put a couple obstacles between us. That second alley spat me out onto a deserted section of road not far from the schoolhouse. I could've tried to hide out there, but it was hardly the second impression I wanted to make on Miss Kane.

Instead, I raced up a small stair set, throwing a passing glance toward the sign. Too quick to make any sense of it. As I twisted the handle and made to slip inside the storefront, I checked the street. The cockeyed kid, out of breath and looking ready to announce my location once more. I wouldn't give him the chance. I stole into the shop and eased the door shut behind me, leaning against it hard enough to keep out a passing horde.

"Young fella," came a voice from behind the counter. "Most of my clientele stops by a little earlier in the morning. All the same, I'd appreciate if you didn't blockade the entrance." Behind the counter sat a woman, maybe ten years my senior. She balanced a small pistol on her lap, and I might've missed it on first glance if not for the small *click* it gave off as she cocked it. The way she held it so casually told me she'd had need to fire it before. Doing so again wouldn't cost her any sleep.

I held up my hands.

She squinted. "You look like you're in an awful rush, my friend. Running, hiding."

"Little of both. I, uh, made some waves the other night, and it seems everybody and their mother wants to chat with me about it. I was just looking for a little peace."

"Well, I guess you found it," said the woman. "Rory Daggett. That's you, ain't it?"

Oh shit. My face must've worn my thoughts, because she went on.

"Don't worry. I ain't going to mob you, ask you to tell folks about my business or nothing like that. Though I admit, I did hope to look you up in the next day or two and talk to you about a certain man up to no good.

You think it's something you can help with, it'd be a boon for us all." She shrugged. "You say fuck it, and you're welcome to sneak out the back door and try to get on home. I won't even shoot you. How's that?"

"Happy to listen."

"Alright, then. My name is Leonora Betts, Mr. Daggett. Although most folks around here call me Nola."

I'd seen the sign over the door that read "Nola's" plenty of times. A tailor. Never paid it much mind. Somewhere in the back of my head was a lonely little place that knew where to take clothing if it ever found itself in need of repair.

Miss Betts, Nola to her friends, offered me a chair and a few minutes to myself while she heated up some water for tea. My head still spun from the noise, the shouting, the odd anger that came from folks rubbing at me like a genie in one of those old Scheherazade stories. Get your hands on Daggett and he'll grant your every wish. Hazel Kane warned me I was famous. She neglected to mention whatever the fuck this was.

I wondered if old Thad was getting the same treatment and let out a soft chuckle, imagining how he'd handle it. Better than me, anyway.

"Something funny?" Nola swept in from the backroom and set two clay mugs on the counter, pausing to watch steam swirl up toward the ceiling, then taking up her own chair again. This time, the pistol in miniature remained out of sight.

"Just thinking about a friend. But what's on *your* mind, Miss Betts?"

"Nola's fine. Don't get all formal and courteous on me. Putting it on the sign is as good as permission the way I see it."

"Fair enough." I sipped the tea. Woody and earthy, but not unpleasant, and with a built-in sweetness.

Nola smiled. "That's the holly you taste. Little different than your standard black tea. Delicious, though. Yaupon."

"Yaupon, alright." Mug to my lips, I let it take another trip across my taste buds. "You didn't invite me to stay so we could talk about tea."

"Nope." She chewed her lip, a gesture that sang out *where to start, where to start.* "So, I guess you must know Sheriff Locke is in charge of organizing an election for a new mayor. Spirit of democracy and all that, he's looking to vet at least two candidates. I've heard your name floated more than a couple times, Mr. Daggett."

"If I'm stuck calling you Nola, then you oughta make it Rory. I didn't know that. Haven't seen Thad in a few days, but it makes sense." I caught myself tapping a staccato beat on the counter with my non-mug hand and dropped it to my lap, where it could patter away without drawing attention.

"You know a man named Alexander Farrell?"

I shook my head, and didn't add how complete a job I'd always done of keeping myself disconnected from Buzzard's Edge without ever actually leaving it.

"He owns the Scarlet Revolver."

"Ah, the Saloon at the End of the World if it was run by the fine folks from Sodom and Gomorrah."

"A little overdramatic, but the Saloon at the End of the World never doubled as a brothel, I'll give you that. And Farrell doesn't try to hide his ownership, nor the fact that he spends the majority of his time there. Separate quarters from the business itself, located on the top floor. Or so they say." She sipped her tea without lowering her eyes from mine. "Fancies himself a businessman. A John Rockefeller type that never found city life. So, what I'm saying is he finances the Scarlet Revolver, profits from it, just never gets associated with the things that go on inside those walls, many of 'em a few feet away from where he dips his pen and signs his papers. Keeping up?"

"So far." That was mostly a lie. I just hoped to stumble upon the equation by the time Nola asked for the answer.

"I had a run-in with Farrell some years back. Ever hear the story about the big goddamn lizard that ran amok just outside town?"

I sat up straight. "A little. I remember my pa running inside our home, slamming the door and jamming a chair beneath the handle. His face was colorless, and Miss Nola, I'm not sure if you knew Henry Taff, but almost nothing on earth scared him, and what little managed to put a fright in him, he never let it have the satisfaction of knowing. This must've been nearly fifteen years ago?"

"Sounds about right."

"He said it was a monster, that it killed a bunch of miners. We stayed inside all day and into the next, playing cards and telling stories. He didn't even go to work. Not for two more days. By then, I guess I'd forgotten all about it."

"Miners. Yeah, that's the one," she said, and a dark cloud dimmed her face. "Look, Farrell didn't make that monster, didn't even let it out of its hiding place, not exactly. What he did was worse, Rory. He heard all about it and just kept sending those men to their deaths. Until it got too big to hide. See, most people never even connected his name to that incident, and those that did forgot about it the next time he put his stamp on something shiny and fun. Money over people. Ain't that always the way?" She chuckled. "I saw through the mask, I paid attention, and I saw a man who'd throw another human on the fire if it kept him that much warmer. Somebody who'd step on your head if it helped him pick fruit off a higher branch. See what I'm saying?"

"Let me guess, he's set his sights on something shiny and fun, like running the town?"

"That's the story. One of 'em anyway. You listen long enough and you'll hear a whole lot more. Nowadays? Let's just say there's a high turnover rate among the girls that tend bed at the Scarlet Revolver, and wouldn't you know it, many of 'em just vanish without a trace once their earning days are staring at the sunset. Sometimes earlier than that. Then there's the johns that don't behave themselves and fail to show up for work the next day."

"Those are some awfully loud accusations, Miss Nola." I licked my dry lips, picked up my mug and found only dregs at the bottom of the cup. "And you planned on coming to me with them. Why's that?"

"You may not know all the folks in Buzzard's Edge, but they know you. Noose and his crew, word is you had something to do with stopping the ice man killings as well, the whole mess up at Devil's Cavern. Dozens and dozens dead, but if you believe the whispers, it could have been worse. And now? A mayor that would murder a child and their pet horse. Look at that, hon. Here you are at the center once more." Nola leaned back and cocked an eyebrow.

"When you put it like that, it sounds downright heroic, but—"

"If you use the word 'coincidence', I swear I will come across the counter and smack you."

My finger continued tapping away at my thigh, so I interlocked it with my other hand and rested them both on the counter while I tried to shape my face into some kind of plea. "Okay, fine, all well and good. I've made some efforts to keep bad people from doing bad shit. That still doesn't make me some kind of brilliant mind that can unmask this guy, trying to line his pockets and put his foot on the town's throat, killing folks who get in his way." I shrugged. "If that's what he's even doing."

She leaned forward and tapped the center of my forehead with an outstretched finger. It wasn't a smack, but it would do. "I'm not after you for your brilliant mind. The man in charge of deciding whether or not Farrell can run for mayor has got that all wrapped up, and I hear he's a friend of yours. No, Rory, I'm asking you because from what I hear if there's anything, *anything*, Farrell's got his fingers in that would make a whole lot of people outside these walls fret, and you and Mr. Locke can find it … Well, you don't really seem the type to just let shit like that go, do you?"

Something heavy plunked in my gut. There'd been a weight there since Ghost died and Alice started avoiding me. Now it had a partner.

Nola finished her tea and clinked the mug on the counter, then crossed her arms and rocked in her chair. She didn't even wait for me to answer. "Yep," she said. "I reckon those chasing you have given up, and you can probably sneak on home, safe and sound. Come back anytime, though, and feel free to bring your little girl. Alice, isn't it? Way I hear it, she's a firecracker and a damn good reason to make this town a little less awful."

"I just might, especially if you promise to keep that tea on hand? Yukon?"

"Not too far off. I'll have it ready to go. You just promise to do me a favor. Keep your ear to the ground. If you hear any rumblings you don't care for, pick your head up and see what's making the ground shake."

Chapter 5

Laws of Chaos

If Miss Nola had given me a clear directive rather than a wagonful of shit to overthink, I might've wound up somewhere other than my bedroom in the farmhouse, staring up at the ceiling and remembering when it used to be made of stars.

That reminded me of Ghost, which made me even less inclined to get my ass moving.

This Farrell guy was supposed to be a money-hungry, power-craving piece of shit who wore a smile when he strolled the streets and banked on just that to land him Mayor Harvey's former position. The way Nola put it, most people didn't even know about his string-pulling abilities and those that did tended to spend dollars and cents that came directly from his pocket. Put another way, they gave a whole lot of hoot about their jobs over their morals.

All of that I could almost live with. The disappearing girls from the Scarlet Revolver, though? Well, that dug under my skin a bit deeper.

Thing was, Nola seemed to know putting a bug in my ear was all but guaranteed to drive me up the fucking wall. High enough to dig into the situation, at the very least.

"Which you cannot do alone," I said under my breath and to no one in particular.

Up I got and wandered into the parlor to find Alice sitting on the couch. She didn't look up when I stepped into the room. A book balanced on her lap made me think of Hazel's suggestion, letting Alice go to school. Several days on, I hadn't brought it up with her, and I feared this wasn't the right time.

Look at her. Reading on her lonesome. What's she need school for?

"I gotta go back into town, Pip. Run some things by Thad, and maybe …"

Maybe what? Keep the town from descending into chaos again? Like I was letting that shouting kid's words get into my head.

Two guns blazing and refused to back down …

"See what he's got to say on a certain matter. You want to come with, or hold down the fort?"

Eyes wandering back and forth across the page, she picked up her free hand, pinched her fingers to her thumb, and dabbed the side of her mouth like she was wiping it with a napkin. Not quite the sign for "I'd rather stay home," but I understood her just the same.

"That's alright," I said. "Probably be dull, anyway."

She made no reply.

Leaning against the doorframe, I kicked at the floorboards and added, "You hungry?"

At this, she looked up, just long enough to shake her head, before returning her attention to her business.

My chest ached, not for the first or fiftieth time recently, and I tried to convince myself that Alice looked just as hearty as ever, and she hadn't thinned out over the last few days.

"Kid," I said. "I know you're going through it. Shit's tough, but you gotta eat. I miss her, too, and it's awful. It's real fucking awful, yeah? But the shit I've seen you knock through and come out on the other side? I'm not saying this is easier, but you're not alone." I chewed my lip. "Try and remember that. And try to eat something. Promise me?"

Gently, and slow as a tree grows way out there in the desert, Alice rested the book in her lap. She lifted a finger to her lips, then dropped that hand to her other, which she'd balled into a closed fist.

Promise.

I might've imagined the glimmer of a teardrop threatening to roll down her cheek. Then again, maybe not. For a moment, all I could do was stand there and watch her. Before I left, I brought my right hand flat off my chest and clapped it against my open left, then pulled the two hands apart like I was ripping a piece of paper. If she noticed, she gave no sign, but I hoped.

Sometimes that's all you have.

A cloud of pipe smoke billowed out when I opened the door to the sheriff's office. The single-room building was hardly palatial but should've been harder to fill with that noxious cloud. Pity the poor prisoners that passed their nights in the cell from time to time.

Locke leaned back in his chair, a pipe dangling from his mouth and his fingers tented on his chest. A casual visitor might observe the scene and peg him as lackadaisical, maybe even so harsh a word as lazy. I knew better. The man was deep in thought over some matter or another.

"Would it kill you to open a window? That East Coast tobacco you order in, it smells like donkey shit dipped in kerosene."

Locke's eyes remained fixed on the nothing they'd been watching when I arrived. "Were it dipped in kerosene, there would be no doubting the aroma, and we'd have yet another building burned to the ground. As for your other descriptor, this particular blend boasts a scent like leather mixed with dry hay. Perhaps that is what reminds you of a donkey."

"No arguing with you. Got a minute, Thad?"

Finally, he turned to meet my eye, which was good, since I'd had almost all I could take of talking to people who barely acknowledged my existence. "Have you come about the mayoral election?"

"Now that's just impressive as hell. How'd you do that?"

A small chuckle, and he shook his head. "For days on end, people have only come in to discuss two topics. How I will be managing this election and the disappearance of Moses Harvey. It strikes me that you would not wish to talk about the latter unless one were to hold hot coals to your feet. Maybe if you'd seen his ghost wandering the streets, though you look healthy, hale, and free of fright." He gestured to an empty chair. "So, I made an educated guess."

Settling into the chair, I took in his office. It was a far cry from the way John Harden, or even Billy Chambers, had left it. Shelves threatened to topple, stacked with books that likely traveled west alongside Locke's tobacco. The "Most Wanted" board hung next to the doorway, right under Thad's hawk-like supervision. No less than eight plants decorated the place, somehow surviving the smoke and lending a blaze of color to the shabby room.

"I've thought long and hard, and I've got no interest in running for mayor," I said. The thinking part was true, the long and hard might've been a stretch.

"Truth be told, Rory, I hadn't considered you as a viable candidate."

I shot him a grin. "What's wrong? Don't think I could hack it?"

"On the contrary." He sat forward and leaned on his desk. "I don't think you lack the ability so much as the desire. Am I mistaken?"

"Seems arrogant to say no." I rapped my knuckles against his desk. "How about this Farrell fella I'm hearing about?"

Thad's eyes became shrewd, his grin widened, and he whispered, "Actually, that is something I had hoped to discuss with you in your unofficial capacity as sheriff's deputy."

A couple months I'd been doing the job, just never put a label on it. I guess it was about time. Sure wouldn't argue with a salary to go along with the title.

"What do you know about Mr. Farrell?" he asked.

"Next to nothing."

If those eyes focused any harder, they might burn a hole through my shirt. After a moment, he relaxed and pulled from his pipe a few times. "I confess I find myself much in the same position. A recipient of murmurs and suggestions, some quite troubling, that hold less weight than a bucket with no bottom."

"Careful, friend, you're starting to sound like you're from around here."

Locke waved the idea away. "I've a notion to learn more and I hoped to solicit your assistance. For the moment, there is another matter I wish to discuss." His face grew deadly serious, and I nodded permission to get on with the questioning.

"The other night," he said, "there was a commotion in the back room of the saloon. You alluded to something I would not be willing to believe. Events took a rather savage turn afterward, and we discussed it no further. I must admit, Rory, it has been on my mind ever since."

So, there it was. Trust the man who stood by me when I told him I saw ghosts? Who watched Alice come back to life in a tub of slime? Something about a monster in a saloon seemed to strain credulity a bit further than even those events, but had it really been any worse than the critters that lurked in the dark frontier?

"Promise you won't laugh. Not even a snicker, alright?"

Locke put a finger to his lips, then placed that palm against his closed fist. A promise and a reminder that the man spoke the language I thought of as belonging to Alice and myself.

"At first, I mistook it for a mountain lion. A cougar. I mean, you saw what was left of Jules. I figured it wouldn't be a far cry for something to smell … well, you know, and slip into town for a meal."

"Wild predators rarely prefer cooked meat to raw."

"You serious right now?"

He twirled his fingers for me to go on and lost himself in thought.

"This wild predator seemed to have no problem with cooked meat. As I was saying, before I was so rudely interrupted, the idea that it was a cougar didn't stick around long. This is the part, Thad. I swear, you so much as crack a grin and I'm out the door."

His face remained impassive. That was alright. I needed to double down, but I hardly needed a second promise from the man.

"It had horns. Like an antelope or a goat. Not only that, it breathed fire, and Thad, let me just swear up and down that it did it twice, and if I wasn't as positive as could be that I saw the fireball come straight from the thing's mouth, I would've kept that shit shut away."

"You shot at it. Several times before you cried out for me. The room was empty by the time I arrived. Where did the creature go?"

I shifted in my chair. "Couple of wings sprung up on its back and it flew out the ceiling."

"I see." True to his word, Locke showed not so much as a hint of a smirk. "An odd question, Rory. By any chance, did you catch sight of the creature's tail?"

"Yes," I said, carefully.

"A serpent?"

A jolt like cold water started in my toes and ran through every inch of me. "How could you know that?"

"Interesting. Rory, I do not discount your experience—far from it—but I wonder, have you considered the possibility of some kind of chemical, not unlike the one you experienced at the hands of Mr. Crane, or his sister?"

I hadn't. The Cranes were out of Buzzard's Edge and trapped in either Hell or some horrifying version of it that rode parallel to our world. Their days of stuffing mad science into vials were through.

With a quick shake of my head, I said, "This was something weird in a familiar setting. In my limited experience, those chemicals fuck everything up. They don't pick and choose."

"Alright, then."

"You going to tell me how you knew about the snake tail?" I asked.

"Not just yet. I've some research to conduct. It would not do to speak out of turn and burden you with nonsense."

Before I answered, I gave it enough breathing room to make him wonder what was on my mind. "Come and find me as soon as you figure it out. Something about this whole game. Feels not quite over. You know what I mean?"

Just like the broken bottles in the saloon. Those laws of chaos again.

Locke had started to form his lips into some kind of answer when a kicked-open door interrupted him.

Despite knowing the owner of the boots very well, she was the last person I expected to see framed in that doorway.

CHAPTER 6

MONGRELS

"Pip," I said, and cut myself short. She didn't look well. Kind of like the sun had bleached her face. Sweat soaked the front of her shirt, and her chest heaved, desperate for breath.

Well, sure, she ran here.

That wasn't it, though. I'd seen that look about people before. It usually meant fever, sickness. Then my rock-solid head came around. Locke got there a split second before me. His voice was flat and hard.

"What did you see?" he asked.

Even with a month between visions, how could I forget? The way her trip to the dark frontier seemed to suck the soul out of her, if only for a minute. I half expected the gray silhouette of her ghost to pop up across the room, and the thought frightened me bad enough to make me shake.

A little color returned to Alice's cheeks as she slapped her hand against her thigh and snapped her fingers. Again. Then a third time.

"We're paying attention, kid. What?"

"Rory," said Locke.

Alice shook her head, hard enough to send her sweat-soaked bangs swinging, then formed her right hand into a claw and held it palm-in toward her face.

That one I knew. And it took less than a second for the first one to click.

"Dog," said Locke.

"Wolf," I shot back.

A momentary look of relief set upon Alice's face, then the first scream from outside knocked it clean off. She went pale again and drew a finger down her lips, toward her chin. A quick swipe up, she laid her pointer against one cheek, then the other.

Red. Eyes.

Outside the sheriff's office, a single animal sauntered down the middle of the street. Under the midday Arizona sun, the thing looked wildly out of place. It was about the size of a runt coyote and had a lot of the same features. A pointed snout and a long canine body covered in bristles of fur so dark it appeared almost blue. Just as Alice warned, its eyes glowed blood red. Besides them, the starkest difference was its gaunt spine, poking out along the ridge of its back like the spikes on a spiny lizard.

I'll be damned, I thought. The red eyes of the nightmarish whatever-the-fuck made me think I mightn't be the one who was damned.

How a creature roaming the streets of Buzzard's Edge could appear so familiar and so strange gave me a moment of pause. Just long enough for Thad Locke to pull up behind me in the open doorway and cock his pistol at the mongrel's head.

"Do you think it's dangerous?" he whispered.

"Kill it!" The sky-high pitch of the declaration helped identify it as the same screamer that had grabbed our attention in the first place. It belonged to a woman in a straw-yellow dress whose ample bosom made it all the more comical that she'd climbed up on the windowsill of Chuck Levy's butcher shop to avoid the creature. From inside, Chuck watched with a look of horror. Maybe at the dog-monster, maybe at the large woman threatening to topple into his storefront.

He wasn't alone. Plenty of souls watched from their windows, not a single one brave enough to set foot on the street. They looked on more with fascination than fright. Hell, I'm sure it was a cheaper show than when the circus rolled through town.

"I don't know what the fuck it is." Shoving my hands down in my pockets, I glanced at Thad. "I mean, it doesn't look all that friendly, but doesn't look too formidable, either." I clucked my tongue at it, and the animal flashed a set of nasty fangs. Long and pointy enough to suggest I pull my hands out of my pockets and have my revolver handy.

It let out a shrill hiss that was halfway to a screech, and the hair on my arm barely had time to stand up before a world-ending boom went off behind me. The dog-thing's throat exploded, spurting a geyser of black blood across the sand. Its back legs jerked a couple times and the gaping hole in its windpipe whistled as it bled out.

A plume of smoke rose from Alice's gun barrel. She stepped forward, ready to follow up if the thing didn't stop trying to draw breath.

"Jesus, Pip. Sure that was necessary?"

She caught me with her icy blue eyes, flash-freezing me with a look like I'd asked the world's dumbest question. The funny thing was, it warmed my heart, because for a second, the girl I hadn't seen in days was back.

From over by the butcher shop, the woman screamed again.

Then something else cut through the air. Close to a scream, only not quite right. In the distance. At least a couple of roads away. The hair on my arms found its way to attention, after all. The sound rattled and hissed like a mule with pneumonia, then shrieked into a piercing hawk-like register.

"Hey Thad?" I flicked my wrist and opened my revolver's cylinder, double-checked that there were six bullets loaded. A quick pat down found a couple dozen more rounds scattered throughout various pockets. "Pip? That thing I said about the first fella not seeming too formidable. That only works if it's by its lonesome. And, uh, I'm not so sure it was."

With practiced efficiency, Alice and Locke checked the loads in their own weapons.

"Aim with care and eschew any shots you are not entirely confident in," said Locke. His gaze traveled up and down the street, settling on some of the occupied windows. "We have an audience I've sworn to protect. Too many stray shots would certainly find me in dereliction of duty." He smiled as if he'd made a joke.

"Don't shoot anything on two legs, Thad. That's all you had to say. Christ."

A river of dust poured from the mouth of an alley maybe forty feet away. Another round of growling shrieks from the stampede headed our way. Five sets of red orbs identical to the ones Alice had just dimmed burned through the clearing dust and we opened fire. One pair winked out as the body behind the eyes, still half hidden by a dust storm, *thumped* to the ground. Another creature jumped over the top with a growl like a phlegmy cough. Thad buried a bullet in its forehead and the spark went out of its eyes.

Three more mongrels burst out of the mire with long, slavering fangs glistening in the sunlight. Alice, Thad, and me, we raised our guns and let them sing like a trained theater troupe, blowing back fur, dark ichor, and shards of bone.

"Well, hey," I said. "That wasn't so—"

The word "bad" almost escaped my lips before the next attack sprang from the side. Clever beasts. At least a sight cleverer than any of us had given them credit for. A second pack raced around the side of the sheriff's office, turning the corner and throwing their bodies like battering rams. One dog-thing that suddenly seemed less small collided with my chest and knocked me over backward. Sand kicked up and my revolver skittered away, lost in the cloud. A shot rang out, and a body clumped, sliding past me like a wagon with its wheels locked. Another gunshot. Then that fucking scream again: the big lady, stretching her lungs and trying out for the lead in Mozart's *Queen of the Night*.

Frantically, I scrambled for my gun, digging in the dirt and coming up empty. Bullets weighed down my pockets. *Well, throw 'em then, Daggett.* Despite the chaos erupting around me, I almost laughed. Then a sharp pain bit into my calf, the same one our mystery shooter had nicked the other night. Needle-sharp and blazing hot. Warm wetness flooded my boot—blood, spit, or both—as the creature that had seized my leg started to shake it. The rest of me rag-dolled along for the ride. I laced my fists together and swung like a hammer in the general direction of the monster, connecting with tough, leathery flesh under a layer of coarse hair. The dog-thing let out a squealing grunt and clenched its jaw.

I swung again, but it was like driving my fists into a hairy stone. Just as I'd started wondering what it would be like to hop around Buzzard's Edge on a single leg, a gunshot thundered. Close enough to make my ears ring. The teeth went slack. Thad or Alice. One of them shot true and afforded me half a chance.

Crawling away like my ass was on fire, I spotted a shimmer of silver among the dregs of dark sand soaked with monster blood, and damn near burst into song when I grabbed onto it and found my revolver. The dust pulled back like a curtain to reveal a few scattered animal corpses and the last three stragglers from the pack drooling and growling. The red in their eyes was intense enough to start a campfire.

Locke and Alice had their guns trained on the surviving dog-things. A shot, this one from Alice, and the one in the middle dropped. With the fallen animal between them, the expression on the other two changed. What I initially took for feral rage became fear. The red in their eyes still blazed, but—

"Hey," I said. My voice was rough and scratchy from rolling around in the dirt. "Hold up a second."

—not because they were angry. Because that was their color. It was how they were born. Just like being pissed off didn't make their teeth sharper or their spines stick up into spears.

Alice kept her weapon steady while Locke turned to me, confusion in his eyes.

"I don't know," I said. An answer to a question no one asked. "Just …" The last two dog-things huddled together, cowering. Had they ever been anywhere near the size of coyotes? I plunked my revolver down into my lap and looked at my compatriots. "Gather 'round, folks. Join the insanity."

Thad followed my lead, lowering his weapon, though he still clutched it tight enough to blanch his knuckles. After a moment, Alice lowered her gun as well.

Granted their stay of execution, the two dogs ran off down the road, returning some of that loose dust into the air, and raced each other toward the open desert. You could almost hear the town sigh.

With relief or disappointment? That was up for debate.

"Just what?" asked Locke, his tone free of judgment. Mostly. Without the impending danger, I got a good look at him and Alice. Ripped patches of fabric lined their sleeves, their pant legs. Dark patches bloomed around them, fresh blood from fresh wounds. Alice had a good-sized cut by her lip to match the old scar on her cheek.

"Animals being animals, I guess. Doesn't feel like they deserve to die for following their nature." I caught Alice's eye and shrugged. "Or because someone gave them an order."

"I'm not sure she would agree." Thad holstered his gun and nodded in the direction of the butcher shop. At the base of the stairs lay the body of the woman. Her pale-yellow dress was barely recognizable with all the blood it had soaked up. Her dark curly hair gathered at her shoulders, shielding from our eyes what the dogs had done.

I swallowed as I remembered shooting into the dust storm.

Hopefully, the dogs.

As if reading my thoughts, Locke trotted over and knelt beside her. "One of them tore out her throat," he said softly.

A relief, quick and cool, swept over me, then vanished as I caught sight of the woman's specter, watching me from the top of the butcher's steps. Her throat appeared intact, though there was a haze of dark blood surrounding it. She said a few words I couldn't make out because the dead rarely know sign language. Then she turned and faded into the wall of Chuck Levy's shop. Probably misted right by the old bastard.

I didn't even know her name.

The words were ready to leap off my tongue when Thad stiffened, like someone doused him in cold water. "Gave them an order," he mumbled to himself. "Rory, do you have reason to think someone sent those things?"

My brain whirred and my tongue stuck in my mouth. *You should've shot those dogs dead* locked in a battle with *you don't do cold-blooded murder.* It took Alice with a wide-eyed inquisitive look and a closed fist tapping her thumb against her lip—the sign for *secret*—to pull me from that stupor.

"Actually, I was thinking about what happened to Ghost. We were just having that conversation about the other oddity that cropped up a few days back. Two new species in Buzzard's Edge in twice as many days. That sure doesn't feel like coincidence." I planted my palms in the sand and winced as my leg complained in capital letters. "Don't suppose you two would help get me up and home, would you? I might be able to put some weight on it, but not just yet."

Locke slung my arm over his shoulder and pulled me to my feet. Alice took up residence under the other arm and helped me to hobble forward.

"Let's get you in the sheriff's office. I …" He looked cautiously at Alice. "I'm sure we can find a way to ferry you home. And I'll need to stay close to the unfortunate victim."

"My life for yours, good sir." I hopped up the steps, then stopped at the top to find my balance. With the biggest shit-eating grin I could muster, I turned to Thad and said, "So, do you believe me now about that fire-breathing cougar?"

Chapter 7

This Sign Means Death

Locke propped me up and set Alice to watch and make sure I didn't do anything stupid, then went to fetch the town's new mortician. A tall fella named Mercer who wore suspenders and a bowler hat. He had blown into town a few weeks earlier. Didn't talk much, just stared around with eyes that seemed to have a story behind them. Not one they were itching to spill, though. Locke and Mercer disappeared for half the afternoon, and when Locke returned, he looked tired and worn.

"No other fatalities. At least none that I can find. Earlene Rowles is in the company of Mr. Mercer and will be laid to rest. Her husband has been informed of the accident." He said it all in the tone of a man reporting on the price of grain. Here are the facts. Make it your own business to assign emotion.

With the news delivered, he nodded and pulled a small tin box from the shelf. For the next twenty minutes, I winced and squirmed like a difficult child as Thad cleaned the wounds around my calf, carefully stitching it in two places. Alice skirted around the room, observing the carnage from every conceivable angle. She grimaced every time I did. Perhaps in disgust at the wound, or maybe just to mock me. Both were real possibilities. After he'd placed the final stitch, Locke stroked his chin, staring thoughtfully at my poor battered leg. Without another word, he disappeared out the back door, returning after a moment with a basket that looked woven together from grass. He dabbed a bit of amber something on the end of his finger and rubbed it into the stitches. "Honey," he said, before I could ask.

"You don't say."

"From the bees. I've started keeping them out back since moving my effects in here." He removed a length of silk gauze from the tin box and wrapped it several times around my lower leg.

Alice curled her hand into a letter C, then let it tip over like she was dumping out a glass of water.

Strange indeed, kid. The whole thing had me stifling a grin.

"Finished." Thad sat back in his chair and let out a sigh so big that he seemed to shrink. "We have much to discuss, and I have neither the energy nor the will to do it tonight. Such matters will keep until tomorrow, I think." He raised an eyebrow. "First thing in the morning. I'll come to you."

"You're a cautious man, Thad. If you say it can wait, it can wait."

"Try to stand. See how it feels."

With a flutter in my stomach—anticipation of another miserable time, I suppose—I inched forward off the chair and set my injured leg down, easy at first, then with a little more trust. "Goddamn. Teacher and sheriff, maybe we oughta make you a doctor, as well. Thad, that's amazing. It's sore and swollen, but it's miles better than it was an hour ago."

"The honey." He laced his hands behind his back and donned a genuine smile, clearly pleased with his work. Maybe more so that it was appreciated.

Not for the first time, I wondered what life was like back east for Thaddeus Locke. What drove him here, and more importantly, what made him stay?

"Do you know Mrs. Ranson?" he asked. "She runs the sweet shop a few doors down."

"Maybe I could pick her out of a crowd, but otherwise—"

Locke waved the rest of the thought away. "She keeps a horse and wagon behind her store. Though she feeds the horse regularly, she rarely uses either. I'm sure she would not be opposed to us borrowing it. Not if it means ferrying the hero of Buzzard's Edge home safely."

I'd almost interrupted him to accept the offer. Until the last bit.

"I appreciate it, but I think I'd prefer to walk." I rocked back and forth on my bad leg to show him it would hold. Hot shards of pain burned throughout, not nearly as terrible as earlier. They mostly served as messengers to tell me I shouldn't walk.

Locke appeared dubious, but too exhausted to try and talk me out of it.

"Thanks again," I said, clapping him on the back. Starting toward the door, I hid each grimace and wince as they tried to peek out past my stoicism. "You coming, Pip? Might need your shooting skills if I have to run from something."

"Yes?" asked Locke. I turned to find Alice tugging at his sleeve. She quickly dropped it, then raised her hand to her face, palm facing in. After a moment, she lowered the hand toward Thad like she was offering something up on it.

A smile curled my lips unbidden. First at the gesture, then at the way Locke's eyes lit up.

"You're most welcome. Both of you." His voice sounded tight. It was the only time I'd ever heard it take on that quality.

It was dark by the time we got home.

The walk was shorter than I figured, and thank goodness for that, because I found myself nervous around each corner, thinking some new monster with sharp teeth and ill intentions lay in wait. Something about using that hero label to borrow the wagon felt wrong. Stupid, but I had my pride.

Alice didn't appear as troubled as me, but her hand never left the butt of her gun.

Without a word, we set to making some dinner. All that gunfire and slaughter will work up quite an appetite. Alice unwrapped a couple hunks of corn bread while I put some pinto beans on the hearth to simmer. She nibbled at her bread, unwilling to wait for the rest as she added a few extra spices to my sparse seasoning.

"You alright?" I asked. The cooking beans popped and sizzled as Alice pretended not to hear me. Another pinch of dried pepper flakes. My stomach would pay later because the kid didn't want to talk to me.

Fatherhood. It's a hell of a thing.

"It was another vision. Wasn't it? That's how you knew to come find me and Thad. You weren't out wandering, saw some red-eyed pups, and just thought you'd give us a heads up. You were white as a barking squirrel's belly, shaking, and it's been a while, Pip, but I remember that look in your eye. You still had it when you walked in the door.

Alice stirred the beans.

"They need a good bit longer. You know that. So, tell me what you saw."

She left the spoon in the pot and walked over to set the bread on the table, then she clasped her hands in front of her, stared down at them, and took a deep breath. When she raised her head, her eyes were like blue fire. A slap on the thigh, a snap of the fingers, and I recognized this sign for what it was this time. Not a flashy way of saying "pay attention," but the sign for "dog." Then she repeated the signs for "red eyes" and, after a quick reflection, added a tap at each corner of her mouth. "Teeth."

Hands expanded outward. "Big."

Fingers extended on her left hand, pretend-pricked by the index finger on her right. "Sharp teeth."

Her breathing sped up as she snapped one hand around the other, then pointed at me, letting that single accusatory finger trail down my leg.

"You saw it bite me. In your, uh, vision. That's why you were so quick to shoot the first one."

Alice nodded frantically and shook her index finger at me. "One more thing."

Her left palm smacked flat against her chest while she brought her waggling pointer finger in front of her face. She tapped it against her chin and curled it into her palm. Lastly, she opened her right hand, wiggled her fingers, and brought both hands together. Then the whole thing again.

"You saw blood. Lots of it." My eyebrows took a leap. "Mrs. Rowles. Must be."

In rapid fire, practiced movement, her right hand tapped her chest, shot to her forehead, then dropped with pinky and thumb extended.

"Of course not," I said. "You couldn't have known. Lordy, Pip." The water burbled, the only sound in the room. After a full minute, I said it again. "You couldn't have known. Was this the only vision you've had since the first?"

She nodded, made a V with her fingers to point at her eyes, then brought it out. The next sign was an odd one. Two hands out. One palm-side up, the other palm-side down, then she flipped them.

"You see death." I said it before I thought about what it really meant. Only two visions, but each one came at the cost of somebody's life. It was enough to build a theory. Getting flashes about things that hadn't happened yet, sometimes far off, and sometimes right around the corner. It sounded like a gift. Surely, there were people out there who would desire such an ability. All it took was one look at Alice to convince you different. She'd saved me. At least that's the way I thought of it. In her head, I expect she felt tricked. Like maybe I was never in mortal danger, and turning her sights on protecting me had cost the old woman her life.

So, not a gift exactly. More like confusion wrapped in a sense of duty, all with no assurance you'll make the right call. Not far off from how I felt about my ability to wave at the silent dead before the underworld sucked them away.

I gave the beans a quick stir and sampled the goods. A tad spicy, but they would go well with the bread. After a hellish day, we might have to help ourselves to an extra chunk. Live like royalty. Two bowls slopped full, and we sat at the table, eating with only the sound of the wandering wildlife outside our window to keep us company. A chipper hoot from an elf owl, distant wail from a coyote, and the soft *skritch* of lizards and scorpions rubbing their way along the desert floor.

A trace of sadness still lived in Alice's eyes, but there were hints of a smile every so often. Sharing a meal while we saved further conversation for another time, it was the most normal I'd felt in a while. There were no ghosts, no trances, and no concerns about either to distract from our unusual little family.

CHAPTER 8

THE HOUSE OF DUBIOUS REPUTE

Alice and me greeted the sun early, knowing Thad Locke would likely do the same, and washed up before downing some coffee and biscuits. As I searched for a jar of fruit to go with it, the jug of sarsaparilla caught my eye. We hadn't had the occasion to try it yet, and I hadn't had the chance to follow up with Hazel Kane for a proper thank you.

Maybe today, I thought with a grin. No sooner had I topped off my outfit with my favorite black hat than a set of wagon wheels crunched through the sand and slid to a halt. A soft nicker came next, and I opened the front door to find Thad Locke at the head of a nice little carriage with patches of wood showing through peeling crimson and gold paint.

"Still works fine," Locke called, as if guessing my thoughts. Knowing Thad, he'd probably read them off my face the same way a man would read a newspaper headline. "Mrs. Ranson was every bit as amenable to lending us her horse and cart as I'd expected. After all, it was I who caught the young bandit sneaking butterscotch drops out of her store without paying."

"You string the kid up?" My gaze wandered toward the horse, a chestnut brown gelding with a crescent-shaped patch of white on its chest. On the older side, but plenty hearty, and with a gentle calm living in its eyes. I walked up slowly and gave him a pat on the muzzle.

"An hour in a cell while I talked him out of future misdeeds."

"Is the punishment supposed to be the jail time or the lecture?" I asked.

"Yes."

A moment passed as the day rubbed its hands together to warm up. "Alice is inside," I said. "If you came to talk, I'd include her. It's been a strained few days since Ghost passed and I'd like to take the opportunity to fill her in on some stuff she's missed."

"Of course." Locke cleared his throat. "Actually, I'd like to talk while we travel, if it suits you. Hence the transport. The girl is more than welcome to join us."

"Ey Alice. Show's on the road," I shouted. "Where are we headed? Should I bring my iron?"

"To the second, one can never be too careful."

I looked toward the door and found Alice framed there, my revolver in her hand and her own in its holster. With a quick flash of the "thank you" sign, I motioned her toward the cart and asked Locke, "How about the first?"

"Have you ever been inside the Scarlet Revolver?" A normal man would smirk when he said it. Thad Locke had the mean gift of keeping anything and everything off his face. Like he was devoting all his energy toward studying your reaction and couldn't be bothered to muster one of his own.

"Never have," I said. Although, of course, I knew of the place.

Alice hopped in the cart and Locke set his eyes forward. "I think it's time we met Alexander Farrell."

He and I rode along in the footboard of the cart while Alice bounced around the rumble. Truly, Thad had a gift for hitting every stone and divot. If he turned that aim to sharpshooting, he could've been even better than Alice.

Once on the road, Thad started in. "Our questioning of Mr. Farrell—"

"Business fella, Pip. Owns the saloon and, uh, house of dubious repute we're headed to. Don't worry about what that means. Okay?"

"—is to be strictly friendly. A sheriff doing his due diligence, and a deputy accompanying him. There is—"

"Oh, yeah. He's also running for mayor to replace Harvey and a woman I met—doesn't matter what her name is, quit waving your hands at me. No, different woman—anyway, she, the first one, says he's bad news."

"—however, the matter of the girl—"

"Alice. No, I'm talking to him."

"—what she might be doing accompanying us."

"Don't worry," I said. "I think I've got that covered."

"As you say," replied Locke, and the conversation lulled for a few streets before Thad opened it up again. "There is the matter of the creature from the saloon, the fire-breathing one."

Alice put her hands up, palms in, fingers spread and made them dance. The word for "fire" performed in such a way that contained an element of "what the fuck?" for good measure.

"One of those things I meant to tell you."

"The body and head of a lion. Not a mountain lion, mind you, but a lion, of the type one would find on the African and Asian continents." Locke spoke like he was reading from a book. "In addition, I believe what you saw had the horns of a goat and a serpent for a tail. And we cannot forget the wings of a dragon."

From the back of the cart, Alice's eyes went from shock-wide to skeptical-skinny.

"Wings of a dragon? Are you—Thad, if you're putting this all together to have a laugh at me, I'm missing the humor."

Locke kept his eyes on the road ahead. "On the contrary. I thought your description yesterday sounded familiar, and though it took a good deal of page turning in the wee hours of the night, I was able to find the creature in question. A chimera."

"Okay, so where are they supposed to live and how far is it from the Sonoran Desert?"

A small, nearly insignificant smile crossed his face, and I wondered again if he was pulling my leg. "To my knowledge, they don't live anywhere. They are creatures that exist only in myth."

We jostled on by the sheriff's office as I tried to get my head on straight.

"If they were to live anywhere," he continued, "it would be on the eastern edge of the Mediterranean Sea, balanced on the line between the European and Asian continents, in a region called Anatolia. To put it succinctly, the chimera caused great havoc there in the old Greek stories. It razed villages and took lives as it pleased, until a hero named Bellerophon finally put an end to it."

With my jaw hanging down by my shirt collar, I caught Alice raising a crooked hand, swiping all four fingers across her head, like she was tracing her eyebrows.

"Thanks, kid. I feel crazy."

She put on a sheepish smile and pressed a fist to her chest, then ran it in a quick circle.

"You're forgiven. How'd this guy Bellafon—"

"Bellerophon."

"Yep, him. How'd he kill the chimera? Seems like we could use that information if you all still believe me, and we're facing down the prospect of more of these monsters showing their ugly mugs in Buzzard's Edge."

"There are different variations of the tale, but the most common sees Bellerophon attaching a molten ball of lead to the end of his spear and forcing it down the creature's throat, causing it to choke to death."

"Jesus." I settled back in the seat and felt the blood drain from my face. "Something to keep in mind, I guess."

With his eyes focused on the road ahead, Locke said, "The girl may speak for herself, however, I believe you. I grew up reading the classics, believing the stories to be just that, stories, but I've seen too many discomfiting things in this new frontier to play skeptic to someone I trust."

I raised my eyes at Alice, and she met me with a thoughtful expression, holding it long enough to wreak havoc on my nerves. Finally, she tapped her index finger against her temple, then clasped her hands together palm to palm.

"Well, thanks." I let a little snark slip into the words to cover the relief I felt in that moment. When you have a time, even a moment, where a good friend or a family member, especially one you found starving half to death in a closet, might doubt your sanity, well, let's just say it makes a man hold his breath tight.

"Hey!" A bit of excitement flooded my voice. "What about the dog-things? You find those in one of your books?"

"Ah, unfortunately not. They do not seem to be from any stories or books on nature I have familiarized myself with." He bit his lip as if to say, *What the hell? We've come this far.*

"I have seen something that may pertain to the matter. My predecessors at the sheriff's office did not keep fastidious records. Most of what I discovered when combing through the stores were handwritten notes, likely scribbled at the behest of a citizen reporting a problem, then shoved aside once that person left. Not to speak ill of Mr. Harden or Mr. Chambers. There was one scrap of paper that appeared a few years old that I've since disposed of. You'll forgive me if I cannot recall the words exactly, but they told of a culling of the livestock on Boden's farm."

"Zeke Boden? Nice fella, but he's a couple ladder rungs short of reaching the top shelf."

"There were a number of other complaints that bore his name, which led me to the same conclusion. This particular one, however, spoke of a group of dog-like creatures that came one night, wandering through the darkness with their bright red eyes."

A chill went up my spine, then died in the heat of the day.

Locke continued, "He fired at them, but evidently missed. The next morning, he found two dead Hereford cows, a mess of slaughtered chickens savaged beyond count, and one dead goat. The goat, he claimed, had puncture wounds at its throat and had been bled dry." A humorless smile formed on his face. "Boden called the creatures 'goat-suckers' in the report."

"Could be something, could be nothing."

"Indeed," he said as the cart pulled up in front of a two-story building with a gaudy wooden sign that read, "The Scarlet Revolver."

Outside the door stood a tall, thin man with a Sharps rifle held at his side. Two bushy orange eyebrows curled in angry examination. They matched his mustache, which seemed even more bold when compared to the suit and bowler hat he wore, which shared their color with chaw spit.

"Business?" he grumbled.

Silently, Locke flashed his badge. The man stumbled back as if shot, then stepped aside and cocked his head toward the door with an ugly scowl.

Before setting forward, Locke eyed Alice and whispered, "What's your plan to get her inside?"

"Okay, ready for it? Step one, we stop referring to her like she isn't standing a couple feet away." I patted him on the shoulder. "Step two, we wing it." I gave the doors a shove and stepped inside.

Every saloon I'd ever visited, which was a small handful, and every brothel, which wasn't, typically opened into a big, cavernous room full of drunk patrons shouting things that were better left whispered, and bawdy music. Even in the calm of the day, these kinds of businesses brimmed with potential energy. The smell of spilled whiskey and dried blood.

The Scarlet Revolver defied the odds by dropping you into a coat-closet-sized room with a counter that looked more like a podium. Behind it stood a door, presumably the entrance, guarded by a fierce-looking woman who probably hadn't smiled since South Carolina seceded. She wore gray hair pulled back in a bun, tight enough to unwrinkle her face, and a floor-length midnight-purple dress. Two stony dark eyes that said winging it had been a bad decision greeted us. Hell, maybe "greeted" wasn't the best word for it.

Good old Thad strolled up and flashed that shiny new badge of his. "Hello, Miss …"

"Agatha," she croaked. Her lips barely moved enough to pass the sound.

"A lovely name. Mine is Thaddeus Locke, the sheriff of Buzzard's Edge."

"We know ya."

"Of course, and I am here to meet with Mr. Farrell about his bid for mayor."

I took a step back and looked around the room. Not much in the way of décor. Four walls that had never known so much as a picture frame and a hardwood floor that only held a passing acquaintance with dust.

And no Alice.

Panic swelled in my gut. She'd been outside with us. Ten feet away.

"Mr. Farrell is not expecting you. He doesn't like to be bothered when he's not expecting people."

As casually as possible with the mounting nerves, I glanced out the double doors. The horse and cart stood tethered where we'd left them. No sign of Alice unless she'd hid in the back of the carriage.

Don't fret now, Daggett. If there's any kid in the wide world who'll be alright alone for a few minutes, it's her.

Then a contrasting voice.

The last time you left her to wait in the streets, somebody put a gun to her head. Remember that?

"Surely, he would make time for the town sheriff. At the very least, would you be so kind to ask?"

Agatha studied him like he was a stain on her tidy floor. "He'll want to know who that is you brought with you."

Locke's voice remained cool as a mountain stream. "Mr. Daggett is my deputy. He is here to act as a witness to all legal proceedings regarding election business."

I had no idea if that was true. It sounded good, though, and more important, it moved Miss Agatha back through her dungeon doorway with a great harrumph.

An interminable couple of seconds passed, just long enough for me to decide there probably wasn't anyone spying on us, and if there was, I didn't give enough shit to fertilize Zeke Boden's barley field.

I hit him with a vicious stage whisper. "Thad, she's gone."

"In the cart?"

Instead of answering, I banged through the batwing doors and hopped up and over the footboard of the cart, scaring poor Mrs. Ranson's old horse half to death. The space in the back was bare as a bone after a buzzard feast. A quick glance up and down the street gave me little hope.

"Forget something?" asked the guard. His scowl had flipped into something that should've resembled a smile and instead looked like a crooked horseshoe.

Lost for words, I ignored him. Passersby eyed me nervously, and I ducked back inside before they could recognize and chase me down the road again.

"Nothing," I said, as Locke met me with raised eyebrows.

"Did you ask the Pinkerton?"

"The what?"

"The man outside," said Locke. "He is new here. Given his mode of dress, I suspect Farrell has hired himself a guard from the Pinkerton agency. Typically, something one does when expecting trouble." He smiled and didn't wait for an answer. "Perhaps she simply got bored and went for a walk. I can go in alone if you wish to search for her."

There it was. A chance to cry off. Guilt poked at my stomach. Reason prodded at my mind.

As if sensing that panic, Locke leaned in. "Far be it from me to give advice to a father, but have you considered giving the girl a little line in which to explore her freedom? She need not be tied to you all the time. And Rory." He raised his eyebrows. "She is armed and hardly fragile."

How a man could be so right and so infuriating all at the same time was one of the great mysteries of the world. I almost had time to try to argue before Agatha threw the door open and said, "He'll see you."

Not even midday and the place had already drawn a crowd. A stump of a man played the piano, light and elegant. Maybe a piece by Chopin. The rowdier music would come later when the drunks turned from quiet and contemplative to boisterous men trying to throw haymakers at the big, bad world around them. A dozen solemn men slouched over the bar, each separated by a stool or more, as if they couldn't bear the idea of human companionship. Not at this hour, anyway.

A group of working ladies gathered in a corner that the lamps refused to touch. Their cat-like eyes followed our path across the saloon, and a hush of voices made me feel a little self-conscious. *One foot in front of the other, Daggett. Just like always.*

"No windows," I whispered to Locke. "That's strange, right?"

He said nothing, but I was sure he'd already noticed. That and a dozen other things that went over my head.

Behind the bar, a bulky fella stood wiping out the bottom of a glass with agonizing persistence. He wore his mustache like a frown. When I caught his eye, I realized I knew none of the men in the Scarlet Revolver. It was as if the place existed separately from the rest of town. Or maybe I'd become more of a hermit than I cared to admit.

I waited for Thad to lead, convinced that as the temporary leader of Buzzard's Edge, he must have known at least a few of the folks under his care.

"Hello," Locke said to the bartender. The man stared back through him and kept on trying to buff a hole through the bottom of the glass. "We're supposed to be meeting Mr. Farrell. Is he here?"

Nothing. Like talking to the backside of a steer.

"Choices are pretty simple, my friend." I stepped forward and tapped on the countertop. "'Yes' would be great, 'no' would be confusing, considering we were told he was ready to see us, but technically an answer, and 'I don't speak English' would clear a few things right up."

The man's jaw clenched like he was chewing cud, and I thought he might be part steer after all.

A titter of voices drifted over from the corner, mostly murky, but one cut through the fog, high and melodic. One of the women. "Aww, quit being such a dick, Lou."

"I don't take orders from the help," grunted the bartender, Lou.

"Fuck you, Lou. You are the help. 'Sides, if Agatha sent 'em in, Farrell's probably waitin' on 'em. You wanna be the reason he gets impatient?"

Something flickered in Lou's eyes. Anger or fear. Whatever it was, he buried it like the law was coming, then grunted again and wandered out from behind the bar toward a set of stairs bathed in shadow. Even took his dirty glass with him.

"Thank you for your assistance," said Locke, tipping his hat in the direction of the voice and jamming his thumbs into his gun belt like he'd been born and bred under the Arizona sun. He flicked his eyebrows into an imploring look and set out toward the table. I followed, knowing it was either that or wait for Big Lou to grump back down the stairs.

The lamp light made an honest effort to stretch across the table, even made it far enough to give me a head count. Three women who no doubt conducted their business in the upstairs rooms once the sun set, and maybe sometimes when it was still beating down.

"Is that Rory Daggett?" The question came from a redheaded woman with freckled cheeks sitting at the edge of the table. Her voice had a lilting curiosity to it, yet somehow the question didn't sound directed at me.

A pencil scratched and leather riffled along the tabletop. Suddenly, the light seemed to grow more generous and reveal the person in the middle to be a little ... shorter than the rest.

"It is," the redhead replied to her own question, peering down at a small journal before she passed it back into the shadows.

Across from the redhead, a blonde girl at least five years my junior leaned across the table. She had cunning green eyes and a blotchy, purple birthmark running half the length of her forearm. "Oh, we've heard all about you. Or, read, at least."

For all his observational capabilities, Locke still hadn't figured it out. His knit eyebrows gave away the game.

The redhead slid over, and I took a seat next to her. "Is that so? Normally I don't care for people talking about me, but when they go to the trouble of, oh, I'm gonna guess sneaking in the back door …" I glared at the small shadowy figure between the blonde and the redhead. "That about right, Pip? Sneaking in to make sure I don't get myself in trouble? Well, I suppose I can make an exception there."

Alice leaned forward into view, a pencil in one hand and a leather-bound journal in the other. She smiled brighter than the lamp light that hesitated to visit this corner. The girls on either side of her giggled and clapped.

Locke laughed hard enough to make the piano player pause. The squat man frowned for a moment before he found the tune again.

"Pip?" asked the blonde once she'd gotten over her laughter.

"Long story," I said. "Just something I call her."

"He's a smart one, Allie. Just like you said. He figured us out, no problem." This from the redhead.

My turn to chuckle. "Allie? I think you mean Alice."

"Yeah, that's what she wrote," said the redhead, "but we like Allie better. Fits her, don't you think?"

Then the blonde chimed in. "Oh, try not to look so pissy, Rory. She's not the first kid that came knocking on the back door looking for her daddy. But, she might be the first we didn't have to distract for five minutes while Daddy searched for his breeches."

The redhead giggled and slapped the table. "She started writing in the dirt. Said she couldn't talk but needed our help to get inside."

"And," said the blonde, "she said I was beautiful, which, as you can see, is both true and got her far."

"Well, thanks for taking care of her and all, but—"

"Oh, I doubt very much she needed us to take care of her," said the redhead.

I turned to Alice. "You couldn't have mentioned this plan to me?"

With palms held flat, Alice crossed her arms in an X-shape in front of her.

"Is that wings? Hysterical. You know you had me worried sick, right?"

"Oh Jesus," said the blonde. "He sounds like my daddy."

Biting her lip to keep from laughing, Alice scratched a few words down before handing the journal to me.

"Vivian," I read. The blonde raised her hand and shot me a buck-toothed grin. "And that must make you Drea."

"It must," replied the redhead. She held out her hand, fingers dangling lazily. "Enchanté."

"Le plaisir est pour moi," said Locke.

Rolling my eyes, I said, "If you kiss her hand, I'm going to leave you here."

"Works for us," said Drea.

"Miss Vivian, Miss Drea. My humble thanks again for getting my disobedient child in here safely. I'm afraid I have to deprive you of the pleasure of her company, though."

"What for?" asked Vivian, with a playful quality to her voice.

"We're to meet with Mr. Farrell," answered Locke.

The light, frivolous feel of the conversation died on the spot. Both women went pale under the dim light.

"You can't tell him we snuck Allie in," said Drea. "Please, I'll do anything."

"We both will. Please, you don't know …" Vivian trailed off and her eyes went distant. "We was just havin' fun. We ain't fixin' to end up like Celeste."

"Or Mina," whispered Drea. "Left out there in the desert, all alone, the ants, they—"

Vivian reached across the table and squeezed Drea's hand.

"Whoa there, hey," I said. "We won't say anything. You have my word, girls."

Vivian and Drea watched us like a pair of mice watching a rattlesnake pass on by.

"Okay," said Vivian. She shot a look at Alice. "She's going up with you? I—"

Drea hit her with an elbow. "You shouldn't have brought her. If I were you, Rory Daggett, I don't know that I'd do that a second time."

"Yeah, okay. Of course," I said.

Vivian took the journal from Alice with a nervous smile as the ladies slipped out from behind the table. Without another word, they slinked past the bar and up the stairs.

A moment passed in nervous silence. Before either of us could say a word, a sharp voice cut in, making me jump. "Well, well, well. Mr. Locke. And you must be Rory Daggett. The whole town's talking about you."

Not too far back, I'd fought a giant. A man whose sole purpose in life seemed to be knocking down walls and breaking bones. In the end, I caved his skull in with a hammer. The man who stood before us wasn't quite that big, but he was every bit as imposing. Something about the fancy, expensive-looking suit that clung to his brawny form said he could ruin your life six ways from Sunday, and if it came down to it, he could probably strangle the life out of you with his bare hands.

"The folks in here call me Mr. Farrell, but you're welcome to make it Alexander."

Chapter 9

Snake Eyes

As Farrell led us toward the shadow-hidden staircase, a few of the patrons I'd previously thought to be in a stupor picked their heads up and glared. Like by following the saloon's owner, we'd done them some kind of wrong. I couldn't put my finger on why it bothered me. I mean, boozehounds often had a surly look about them, that was kind of their thing, but this group wore expressions on their faces like someone had swapped their drinks out with fresh piss.

A strange, stupid thought intruded just then. *What if they were stone sober to a man, revolvers hanging by their sides, ready to deal death if anything went south?*

For the moment, I put the question out of my mind and ducked into the dark. As expected, the stairs led up toward the second floor. A loosely hung bit of rope closed off a second set, which descended into a root cellar or something similar. Hopefully not anywhere Farrell's people had to spend any prolonged time because a stink rose from there that I was glad to move away from. Jarred goods for the saloon, maybe. Long past their prime if they were ever any good to begin with.

The reek scratched and clawed at my nose even as we climbed away from it, me shepherding Alice up the stairs behind Thad. As convinced as I was that Agatha wouldn't have let the kid in, once she found her own way, nobody seemed to care one way or the other.

The top of the stairs opened up to an immense hallway, lavishly decorated with a running carpet the color of the saloon's namesake. Between each closed door stood a mirror or a vase of purple salvia flowers.

Something sweet to cover the smell of sex.

The thought darted through my mind, no doubt spurred on by the muffled groans and grunts emerging from behind several of the doors. A little early in the morning for my taste, but to each their own.

At the end of the hall, Farrell reached into his vest pocket and took out a key.

Before he could jimmy the door open, a naked man busted into the hallway, johnson swinging like a breeze had found its way down the hall. A trickle of blood ran down his forehead, which he must've used to open the door, since his wrists were handcuffed behind his back.

"Help!" cried the man, and I have to admit I didn't quite know what to do.

From the broken-down doorway, a lady with long curls of black hair trailing down and covering her unmentionables leaned out. Bare as Eve, she held an object I didn't recognize, but no doubt one she'd used to strike the poor gentleman, all while charging him for the pleasure.

"Excuse me," said Farrell, stepping past us. His eyes popped open at the sight of Alice trailing behind. "My word. This is no place for such a … a young woman."

The walls all but shook as he stomped down the hall, grabbed the handcuffed fella by the shoulder, and tossed him back through the broken doorway. Farrell offered a hapless grin before shutting the splintered wood behind himself. More flesh smacking flesh sounded from behind the doors, behind the walls. Somehow, it seemed a bit more sinister this time around.

"You going to do anything about that?" I whispered to Locke.

"At the moment, I am not witnessing a crime."

A moment went by before Farrell shoved the wreckage of the door aside and stepped out into the hallway. He straightened his collar, called out, "Get Owen to clean up and take the rest of the afternoon off, Evie," and set back in our direction.

"How 'bout now?" I elbowed Thad.

"Sorry about that." Farrell unlocked the door to his office, pushed it open, and cleared his throat. "I'll have to speak to Agatha about allowing the girl in."

"There's a funny story about that, actually." I brushed by Farrell and helped myself to a padded leather chair in front of a desk that was too large to have been carried up the stairs in one piece. Alice sat on one side of me, Locke on the other, and after a moment of waiting for that story, Farrell sighed and settled himself behind the desk covered in clutter, mostly papers with a few random items thrown about. A bullet with no pistol in sight, a leather-bound book, a couple empty glasses, and some loose coins. He folded his hands, laying them on the only empty spot big enough for them. It seemed he might offer us a drink, but he neglected to play gracious host.

"Mr. Locke, or should I say *Sheriff?* I do hope my papers were in order. My sincere apologies for not delivering them myself. Oftentimes, keeping to my schedule requires me to delegate certain assignments to a hired hand."

Farrell's voice came out thick and syrupy, each word carefully chosen.

"They were, indeed," said Locke. "Consider this a follow-up so that I might make a final decision as to the propriety of each self-appointed candidate."

I watched for a flash of anger to spark in Farrell's eyes. Instead, they went dull. Snake's eyes. I met his gaze as best I could. "As a citizen of Buzzard's Edge, Mr. Farrell, one would hope that keeping to your schedule wouldn't require delegating important mayoral duties to a kid with his daddy's too-big boots and a nasty batch of pimples."

Poke the snake and he just might stick his tongue out.

Farrell only smiled. "Mr. Daggett." He raised a hand to stifle any reply. "Yes, of course I know you. The hero of Buzzard's Edge. You're not here to announce your campaign in opposition to my own, are you?"

Alice raised a single eyebrow. No sign necessary. *Are you?*

"Well, I'm not all that interested in running things here, only making sure that whoever does, runs things better than the last guy."

"Mayor Harvey always did a fine job," said Farrell.

"Awful lot of witnesses that might disagree with you there. Three of 'em in this room alone." A few seconds of silence crept in. No admonishment, only an intrigued gleam lit in his eye. "So how about it, Mr. Farrell? From the man that runs the law enforcement side of things around here, the fella that helps him out from time to time, and the youth of Buzzard's Edge who stands to inherit the chessboard we set up, why are you the man for the job?"

Farrell chuckled, a deep sound that felt designed to mock the person who drew it out of him. He took off his suit jacket and draped it over the back of his chair. His white button-down shirt, sweat stains collecting at the underarms, strained to keep his bulk contained. Some of it was slabs of muscle, sure, but not all. It was the kind of body you developed when you couldn't be fucking bothered to walk a stack of papers a block over to the sheriff's office.

"Why am I the man for the job?" he repeated. "Well, first and foremost, I'm well versed in running things. A mayor shouldn't be afraid of a little multitasking, and a lot of money management." He glanced around his office, understated but undeniably sophisticated. Shelves lined the walls, mostly full of books, arranged with care. The way you might set up an office when you're more concerned with how the books look than what's in them. "Many men in the city are, or have been, in my employ. Surely, they can vouch for my management skills."

Because they're satisfied or because they're afraid not to?

"Women too," I said. "Would you say they're all happy the way you run the ship?"

"Rory," said Thad under his breath, somehow shrinking my name to a single syllable.

I smiled politely. "Consider the question withdrawn."

With a nod, he continued. "A mayor needs to be willing and able to make difficult decisions. That much has never been a problem for me."

"Yeah, I guess we just saw that in action. That fella down the hall gonna be okay? Looked like that cut on his head didn't have much blood to spare."

Farrell's face remained blank. When he spoke again, he continued like I'd never interrupted. "Lastly, I suppose, because I know what I'm walking into." He looked down at his hands, as if surprised to see them there. "I've some ideas on new ordinances surrounding business practices, public behavioral expectations, and other such matters. When the time is right, I would be happy to expand on them." He licked his lips. "And, of course, the mayor must also ensure there is a sheriff in place. Mr. Locke, I mean no disrespect, but you were handpicked by Moses Harvey. From what I can see, you have done a respectable job in the interim. I should hope further investigation would result in a permanent home for you down there in the sheriff's office, if you so desire, but I think we both want what's best for the town. Am I correct?"

"Be a shame if your candidacy papers found their way into a hearth fire," I said.

"Rory." Another sharp warning from Locke.

"Wouldn't surprise me," said Farrell. "From what I hear, you're quite the talent at finding ways to make things go up in flame. Not to worry, Mr. Daggett. A savvy businessman always keeps extra copies of important documents on hand."

Snake eyes, I thought, and maybe that wasn't quite right. A coyote. Baleful, disassociated, and a hint of cunning, all hidden behind one hell of a poker face.

Farrell went on, "No, I certainly don't mean to sound like I plan to upend the things that are running smoothly. I do not wish to let you go,

Mr. Locke, and I suspect I won't have to, though I may have to reassess the number of deputies you require to do the job."

Good work, Daggett. That's what happens when your mouth has a looser cylinder than your six-shooter.

I almost let the anger show on my face, then I remembered the job didn't pay, and I let the fucker have his smirk. "You talk like you've already got the job, Mr. Farrell. There's still an election to be held. My, my, I sure do hope the people of Buzzard's Edge share your vision."

Farrell cleared his throat and mirrored my smile. "In my experience, unopposed elections are not all that difficult to win."

I did a less decent job of hiding my reaction to that.

"Thad?"

He graced me with a look that confirmed Farrell's claim.

"You're awfully quiet, Mr. Locke." Farrell's mouth straightened out.

"My deputy, acting as the town's representative, I might add, seems to have touched on all the matters that occupied my mind. There is nothing further from me, Mr. Farrell. From any of us." He stepped on that last sentence. With a small bow, he added, "I will be in touch if I need anything further, or to inform you when an election date has been set."

Farrell stretched his face into a toothy smile, the kind that would look awfully good beaming at the townspeople when Locke had to announce his win. Maybe when he had to smile before a real audience, he could find a way to let the grin touch his eyes. Without looking away, he snatched some papers from the corner of his desk, shuffled and tapped the stack to even them out.

"I trust you can find your way out? Through the front entrance this time, I think." He glanced at Alice, and I realized it was the first time he'd acknowledged her since the hallway. "Oh, and Mr. Locke … or Mr. Daggett, you are welcome to help yourself to one of the women before you leave. On the house. If you can find a nursemaid for the girl, that is. If not, I'm sure my staff can put Alice to work. Keep her busy."

Damn near a quarter century living in the desert, and I can confidently say I'd never gotten that hot before. My cheeks burned like dry brush in wildfire season and my revolver tugged at my hip, begging to be drawn.

Then a thought tamed the blaze.

The kind of man that would let you walk into his office without taking your weapon is either wildly stupid or has a plan.

Farrell did not strike me as a wildly stupid man.

Slowly, and with a hand trying its damnedest not to shake, I touched the brim of my hat and stood. "Thank you for the offer, Alex, but we've got places to be. I'll have to decline. Courteously, for sure."

He held the stack of papers and watched me, a dab of sweat gathered along his mustache. There was a gun within reach of him. I could almost smell it. The second I grabbed for my revolver, I'd be bleeding out on the man's carpet before I knew what hit me. Given the crimson color of the rug, I might not even be the first.

"I, also, must decline your generous offer." Locke spoke in a stiff manner, catching me off guard. He'd all but flooded the office with his silence since our arrival.

"But I'm sure we'll meet again," I said, and turned to leave. A bullet-sized spot itched between my shoulder blades. Deep down, I knew Farrell wouldn't shoot me in the back.

Not today, anyhow.

Down the hall, past the slapping bodies that each door hid—*keep her busy*—past the open room. No blood, no body. My feet padding along the carpet. Don't stomp. Don't even frown. Keep your face clear of emotion. Hands by your side. Nope, in front. Away from the gun. Don't give anyone a reason. Alice tap-tap-tapped behind me, somehow hitting every exposed patch of hardwood. And there was even carpet on the stairs. I didn't notice that the first time. That was alright. Keep my own footsteps quiet. Keep them from drawing any attention. Any more attention. I don't know what Locke did. I couldn't bring myself to look anywhere but straight ahead. At the base of the stairs, that stink jabbed at me again. Not spoiled food, that wasn't right. Shit, death. Like they'd turned the basement into a jakes and let a slew of rats drown in it. How in the fuck do you conduct a business with that smell wafting into the saloon? How do you fuck with the smell of shit creeping in under the door? Past the bar, Big Lou still washing that fucking glass. Goddammit, Lou, if it's not clean yet, it ain't going to find its way there. Figures tucked away in the corner. Maybe Drea and Vivian, maybe not. Laughter. Glares. The gents who scowled as we made our way upstairs hung out and waited in the light for us to come on back so they could glare some more. Take a good look, assholes. I ain't going to give you nothing. Keep your face clear. No expression.

Don't speak.

Don't say a fucking word.

Don't let them know they got to you.

So many of 'em just vanish without a trace once their earning days are staring at the sunset.

Wasn't that what Nola had said?

Out of the gloom and past Agatha. Head down, she ignored us like she still mistook our trio for a nasty spot on her entrance floor. No soft padded steps out there. *Click, click, click* all the way across the small room, out the batwings, and into the sunshine. Don't even look at the Pinkerton, you might knock his teeth out before you realize what a bad fucking idea it is. Keep going. But it wasn't far enough because Farrell's room had a window, a balcony, and if he really was busy, then I was a senator. No, he'd be watching. And that was alright, because I wouldn't show a damn thing. Up the street, sand and dust crunched under my boots. Past one side street, two. Some stares. The hero of Buzzard's Edge, indeed.

"Rory, are you—"

"Not now, Thad." The words came out just above a whisper, and I slipped into the next alley, took a couple steps, and let out a scream as I drove my fist into a stone-hard chunk of wood holding up the walls to Mrs. Ranson's sweet shop. My fist throbbed, and I shook my fingers free. Maybe honey could cure that, as well.

"Rory," he said again. He put a hand on my shoulder. I was trembling all over. Part of me wanted to hit the wall again, like the next time would make a dent. "If it is any consolation, I commend the remarkable restraint you showed. I do not know that I could have done the same."

I nodded without looking at him and cradled my fist. "How do you give a kid that extra line, that freedom, when there's so much awful shit out there?"

He didn't give an answer, and I didn't expect one.

At the mouth of the alley, Alice stood silhouetted against the sun. Slowly, she lifted her right hand, all five fingers extended, turned it sideways, and tapped her thumb to her chest.

I laughed, couldn't help it. The vocabulary that girl had mastered, she could've said a thousand and one things. *Asshole. Kill him. Stop him. Don't punch walls, idiot.*

Instead, she went with "Fine."

A single syllable word, and I could read all manner of things into it. That she was fine, or she would be. Or that I was fine, and to stop being so dramatic. That everything would be fine, because we'd tussled with some real bastards before, and we had it in us. Maybe all those things at once.

She took a step into the alley and held up her free hand. Something caught the light as she unclenched her closed fist.

"What's that you got there, Pip?"

In answer, she dug her thumb under the shiny metal piece and flipped it toward me. Locke snatched it out of the air and studied it in that cunning way he had. A moment or so of meticulous concentration, then he nodded and paled.

"Where did you get this?" There was no anger in Locke's voice. In fact, there wasn't much of anything.

Alice crossed her arms in front of her chest and hooked the fingers of her right hand against her left elbow before dragging her fists toward each other.

"From Mr. Farrell's desk." Not a question. The sly hint of a grin crept onto Locke's face. He held up the object to me. A coin. No bigger than the eye of a rifle and almost certainly made of real silver. I stepped forward to see it better.

Set dead center was the image of an animal I'd seen only once before. A lion with goat horns, a snake tail, and dragon wings. Locke had called it a chimera, and Farrell evidently knew a little something about them.

I'd have to ask him all about it the next time we got together.

Chapter 10

A Couple of Song Dogs

After a little awed discussion, we set out in separate directions. Locke walked back toward the Scarlet Revolver to retrieve old Mrs. Ranson's horse and cart, which, in my haste, I'd forced us to leave behind. Alice and me, we made our way toward Nola's tailor shop. It was near midday, her self-proclaimed downtime.

Locke's parting words echoed through my head as I led Alice through the shadows, hat pulled low to avoid drawing attention. He'd told me that Farrell wasn't lying about running unopposed, and just the fact that the saloon owner knew that and was unafraid to share it with the town sheriff had a lot of wide-ranging implications. Fear on the part of any who might step forward, or perhaps something as simple as bribery. So, what we needed, said Thad, was someone unafraid and not for sale.

"And I know just the man." He'd clapped me on the shoulder and flipped me the chimera coin before heading on his way.

If people didn't stop telling me to consider a run for mayor, I might grow dumb enough to actually listen.

"Rory!"

Hazel Kane jogged to catch up with us, practically beaming with excitement. "And you must be Alice." She balled up both fists in front of her chest, then tipped them over to point at Alice. "How are you?" she asked alongside the motion.

Alice, the girl of a thousand words, shot back the well-worn gesture for "fine."

"You studied up," I said. "She says 'fine', by the way. Not much of a talker, that one." I cleared my throat. "Alice, this is Miss Kane. She was by the house the other day, brought us some sarsaparilla that I am just realizing we haven't tapped into yet. My apologies, Miss Kane. Been a busy couple of days." My cheeks heated up and I doubt it had anything to do with the sun.

"So I've heard. Well, it'll still be alright when you get around to it. And yes, I did study up. Only a little, but if I'm to potentially bring in a new student, I like to take every advantage to get to know them before they enter the schoolroom."

Scratching at the back of my neck and somehow going redder, I said, "Ah, on the subject of things I forgot to do …"

Hazel's eyebrows jumped and a very schoolteacherly look cracked off in her eyes. Honest to goodness, it brought back memories of the swift brush of cane on ass when I halfway'd my mother's lessons.

"But there's no time like the present," I said. "Pip, Miss Kane thinks it might be good for you to join in with the other kids and learn the stuff I can't teach you from somebody who knows what they're doing."

Alice scowled and held a hand out, clapping her pointer and middle fingers to her thumb a few times and shaking the whole sign back and forth.

"Well," I said to Hazel's knit eyebrows, expectant smile, and lovely countenance, "she says she'll think on it."

Raising her eyebrows in what I can only assume was indignation, Alice brought all four fingers to her thumb and waved it around in front of her chin. If Hazel Kane knew the sign for "liar" she gave no indication.

"I admit I haven't gotten very far in my studies. What did that one mean?" she asked.

"Oh, she's just being funny. Uh, Miss Kane. Hazel. We are in a little bit of a rush, so how about we continue this talk another time?"

Those soft brown eyes lit up like someone had sparked a fire behind them and brought them to life. "I don't mean to be forward, but are you courting me, Rory Daggett?"

Any trace of anger had faded from Alice's eyes, replaced with amusement.

"Do you … want me to court you?"

Nice one, Daggett.

"I'll tell you what. How about I come by a night and we'll cook something up, the three of us, and talk further." She laughed. "You can go on your way and get inside. Judging by your face, Rory, you've had too much sun today. Would tomorrow be alright?"

I looked at Alice, like a nine-year-old might have plans. She rubbed her right palm against the back of her left hand, the sign for "busy."

"I agree, Pip. Sounds perfect. Need me to pick up anything?"

"Don't you dare," said Hazel, starting to walk away. "I've got something in mind. I'll be by a little before sundown. Tomorrow." She said it again with an ear-to-ear smile.

Alice rolled her eyes and crossed her arms into an X, giving herself a squeeze.

"You've got to stop doing that every time I talk to a lady. Maybe I just want a friend more my height."

With a near-silent squeak, Alice let out one of those laughs I loved and gave me a hug.

"Come on in, Pip. You're going to meet Nola Betts."

"Got any more of that tea I like?" The store was empty except for Nola wiling away the hours behind that counter of hers.

"That and the gun, hidden just out of sight. You're welcome to either one, Rory." She smiled, mostly to herself, and sat up in her seat. "And this young lady, you'd be Alice?" Nola settled an appraising look on Alice, swept her from head to toe and back again. "Strong hands, long fingers. You've got lean muscle that speaks of hard days, darlin'. You ever want to learn a trade, you come see me and I'll show you how to make a stitch that even your daddy can't tear in all his rip-roaring gunfights and rundowns on the streets of Buzzard's Edge."

Alice looked at her thoughtfully, then to me. She pointed to herself, then twisted a figure eight on her chest with her thumb touching her middle finger, and finished by pointing at Nola behind the counter, all with a subdued smile on her face.

"She says she'd like that," I translated.

Alice appeared pleased that I wasn't misrepresenting her words again.

"And why do you sound surprised?" asked Nola.

"Just Alice doesn't always take to new people. This ain't the first or second offer she's gotten today, but it's the most well received."

Nola nodded. "We'll figure something out, then. But Rory, you didn't come in to get your girl a job, or to drink up all my tea. That right?"

"No, ma'am." I took off my hat and held it in front of my chest.

"Well, sit on down, and cut the ma'am shit. Talk to me, Daggett."

"We're just coming from a visit with Alexander Farrell, and not to put too fine a point on it, but I don't care for the man."

"Tell me."

I did. Everything from the Pinkerton out front to Vivian and Drea's mysterious friends, whatever might have happened to them, to Farrell's parting comment about Alice.

Without so much as a cup of tea before me, I clamored on and when I finished, the sun had shifted its position in the sky. Not a single customer had interrupted my story, and I felt a pinch lighter. Like Farrell's words had curled up in my chest, a little black ball of filth that weighed as much as a bag of horseshoes. All it took was a little pissing and moaning to unload that shit. Alice nodded along to the beat of the story, focusing on her boots all the while. Nola watched the light trail down the wall the whole time, still except for the rise and fall of her chest.

When I killed the story's spigot, all she said was, "That sounds about right. Arrogance. He mighta killed that naked john right on the other side of the door from you, for all you know." She sighed. "All those years ago, I had a talk with him, the kind that happens at gunpoint. Figured maybe I scared a little sense into him. He kept his businesses going, and I heard rumors and whispers. Those tend to be quieter than shouts, however, and there were none of those. Nope, sounds like the same old bastard who shoved his men down a mineshaft with a monster at the bottom to make a couple more dollars. And it's no accident that no one'll step in to oppose him. You know that, right?"

I waited for her to suggest I run against him as well. She may have thought it but didn't let the words out.

"Ask Locke what kind of salary the mayor draws. I'd wager it's piss and rocks compared to what that saloon must pull in. Which leaves two options for why a man in his position would commit to such a thing. Firstly, he's a generous soul who wants to see his hometown prosper and believes he alone can make it happen. And without that fucking arrogance, he probably could've done a halfway decent job of convincing you and Mr. Locke of that."

"I'll say." I snuck a look at Alice and found her gaze shifting between her own shoelaces and the woodgrain of the floorboards. She looked uninterested. That wasn't it, though. She was listening, maybe making some plans. "Second?" I asked.

"Well, second makes the most sense. To me, at least. Problem with the second is, it still leaves us guessing. I'd say he's got his eye on some kind of gain, and the mayor's office gives him the power to acquire it for hisself. He can appoint folks, maintain power over the sheriff's office, as he was only too happy to tell you, manage the town's finances, and I s'pose there's some other duties that Mayor Harvey never bragged about. I just don't know what they are. Hell, when you're hashing out the salary thing with Locke, find yourself a full list of mayoral privileges. With any luck, something'll jump out and give you a place to start." She shrugged. "Could be as simple as he's got his fingers in a pie he doesn't want anybody else knowing about. Those missing girls come to mind again; that's for sure. I mean, what better way to skirt the law than to oversee it?"

She grinned like she'd just thought of something funny. Alice picked her head up.

"I'm glad you got a good read on him, Rory. Seems more than a few people have had the wool pulled over their eyes by that snake. Maybe ignorance, maybe just the good old American dollar. And speaking of snake, I think your first read on him was correct. He's a goddamn serpent." She held up a hand to silence a retort that wasn't forthcoming. "I get how you arrived at coyote, some folks believe they're sneaky beasts that live to pick the bones of lesser critters. It's not untrue, I guess, but in their own way, they're noble creatures. You ever hear 'em called song dogs before?"

"Can't say I have. Got a ring to it, though. Didn't realize I was talking to a critter expert."

"There's a difference between being an expert and listening when people talk. The latter is most of my day. Song dog comes from what the Aztecs down Mexico way used to call 'em. They howl, yip, bark, and even hiss. Folks'll say it's how they have a conversation, and I'd say that's just about right. Makes 'em a little closer to human than they get credit for. But I'll tell you what they can do that most people don't know. That big ol' stock of sounds, what it's really useful for, is a group of two can make themselves sound like seven or eight. Fierce little creatures, they are, but a hell of a lot smarter than most people believe." She shook her head. "Nah, that Farrell is a snake. A reptile soaking up the sun and waiting for an ankle to bite. Don't let him fool you into thinking he's more sophisticated than that, Rory."

I chuckled and wiped my hand across my mouth. At first it was an effort to cover up the laugh, then I thought, fuck it, Nola wasn't one to take offense. "You know," I said. "I used to tell Alice here that we were like a coyote and a vulture, two of the heartiest, meanest creatures wandering around the territories, and maybe we are."

"Or," said Nola, "maybe you're just a couple of song dogs."

"A little closer to human than people want to give us credit for."

"*Mmhmm.* Tell you what, I don't know that I've got anything else to say that'd be helpful at the moment. But you unearth anything else interesting, you bring it here first, you hear?"

"I will, and if your offer to take Alice on was sincere, we can revisit that when this whole mess gets a little closer to wrapped up."

"Oh, it's sincere as the night is chilly. You come back anytime, girl. In fact …" She climbed to her feet, and the chair groaned. "Let me send you on your way with a couple mugs of tea. Then you have to come on back and return 'em."

That was alright.

Chapter 11

The Girl From Brigsby

Just as the sun started to paint the sky in brilliant shades of pink and purple, Hazel appeared in the shadow of the town, a basket held under her arm. She wore a daisy-yellow dress that made me think for a moment of Mrs. Rowles, chewed to death in the streets by one of those goat-suckers, as Locke had called them.

I blinked away the memory and forced a smile onto my face. The last few days had blown by, leaving me little time to do much besides breathe and shoot. Hell, I'd asked a woman to come by the homestead before giving due consideration to whether that was something I wanted. However, the sight of Hazel in that dress made my mind up in a hurry.

It wasn't the way it clung to her hips, though I liked that too. No. A couple little spots of blush lit up on her cheeks when she caught my eye from across the yard, almost like an embarrassed way of asking, "Did I do alright?"

"You found the place," I called.

"A little bit of a search the first time, but once you know what to look for …" She trailed off and pulled up to a stop, holding the basket in front of her and keeping just out of spitting distance.

I smiled and said, "I guess I've been looking forward to this," then realized it was true. "Please, come on in. It ain't much, Miss Kane, but it's home."

"*Isn't* much," she said. The hint of color on her cheeks turned rose red, making that scar by her nose glow like sunlight, and she started up the steps. "And I'd like it if you called me Hazel. Will you?"

"It *isn't* much, but it's home." I clucked my tongue. "It's like that, huh? Hazel."

"How could I look my students in the eye if I let a grown adult get away with such grammatical abominations?"

Once inside, she looked around. My gaze followed hers and I fretted over every speck of dust and found items on the floor I'd swear hadn't been there minutes earlier.

"Is Alice here?" she asked.

"She's kicking around somewhere. Once she smells things cooking, she'll float on out here, I'm sure."

Something lit in Hazel's eye. Maybe disappointment, maybe something I was too out of touch with the ways of women to read. "Uh, pans are ready to go," I said, "and I'd be remiss if I didn't help you get things ready. I won't pretend I'm great in front of a hearth, but I'm at your disposal."

While the sky shifted from pink to red to a dark blue and eventually black with thousands of little white pinpricks, we chopped up potatoes, seared some cuts of beef she'd brought, and put on some homemade sourdough biscuits to brown, all the while asking the kinds of useless questions you're supposed to ask when you're trying to figure out if you want to keep a conversation going or shovel down your food and call it a night.

Her favorite book was *Treasure Island.*

She grew up just outside of Oklahoma City. A dusty little place called Brigsby. Played the violin when she was little but hadn't kept up with it.

Liked dogs and wanted to get one once she got a little more settled.

Never planned on being a teacher until the opportunity fell into her lap, and she discovered a knack for it.

Also, her father had died in a wagon accident when she was eleven. I nodded and offered sympathies, but held my own tongue, not quite ready to share my own version of that story. I couldn't help thinking she was half an orphan and she'd fit right in around here. Part of me hoped Alice was listening in. A tragedy like that wasn't quite having an outlaw kill your parents right in front of you. Still left scars, though. You could tell by the way Hazel brushed her finger by the side of her nose, probably not even aware she was doing it.

At some point, Alice drifted out from her hiding spot. Hazel and me only noticed when her shadow crept toward the hearth, approaching just as I sampled one of the taters to make sure it was done. A few quick and practiced flicks of the hand, and Hazel managed to ask how she was doing and tell her it was nice to see her again.

And dammit, Pip softened, right then and there. You could watch her chin slowly rise up and the suspicion drain from her eyes.

I never asked her, but I suspect it wasn't necessarily Hazel's effort to learn a bit of our language. Yeah, it surely took some effort, but five minutes would do it. No, it was the progress. That she approached Alice with a bare understanding one day and continued to flesh it out the next. And isn't that the kind of person you might welcome into your life? The kind that thinks about you when you're not around.

We ate in relative silence, Hazel and Alice passing signs and ignoring me. That was alright. Watching the scene could almost pass for entertainment. Alice's signs had started moving at cyclone speeds in the year or so since we'd started working out of our sign language book. As practiced as I was, even I had to ask her to slow down sometimes. With Hazel, she kept to simple signs, only stringing phrases together on rare occasions, and even then, waiting until Hazel had grasped one sign before moving to another. A couple times I jumped in when the two got stuck. Hazel focused on individual letters and the ability to resort to spelling hauled them out of a few jams. Mostly, I just shut up and tried not to show Alice how much I was enjoying it.

Then a thought struck me.

Hazel was going to ask about putting Alice in school. Build up a rickety bridge, then try to cross it with a jug of kerosene in one hand and a lit match in the other. Only the question never came. Another night—and I kind of hoped there might be one—and it likely would.

When everyone was good and stuffed, Hazel patted her knees and stood. "I'd best be going," she said. Her eyes said the quiet part. She didn't want to walk back into town in the middle of the night and let those watchful eyes occupying every window guess where the single young lady was coming from. If she'd said as much, I might've added that they wouldn't have to guess. They already knew, and even the fact that a kid was present wouldn't save her from flapping lips.

Alice put her right hand to her chin, then brought it forward, cupped it in her left and bounced them both back to her chin. Two signs that were made to work together.

Thanks for the grub.

Hazel returned the sign for "thank you." Another marvel because you didn't learn that people said, "thank you" and "you're welcome" the exact same way without spending a bit of time looking into it.

Alice cracked half a grin and retreated to the shadows. Hazel started gathering up the plates, and I waved her away.

"I'll take care of that," I said. "How about I walk you out?"

"I'd like that." She gathered up her basket and took one more look around, less like she was inspecting the place and more like she was trying to commit it to memory.

We stepped out onto the porch, and I shut the door behind me. The night was cool and still, no kick to the air. "I had a nice time," I said. "And my adoptive mother would strike me down from heaven for this, but I don't remember the last time I had potatoes that sang quite like that."

"Coriander."

"You don't say."

"I do." Her eyes darted toward the horizon, then came right back. "You two ever get around to that sarsaparilla?"

"Not for lack of trying. Once the world slows down a little."

"I made the jug myself. Pottery is a hobby of mine. Something to do in my free time. Keep busy, you know?" She sighed before I could answer and licked her lips. "She's a smart kid, a good kid. Whatever you've been doing with her, it's admirable."

"So, you don't want her in the class anymore?" I put on an extra-large grin, so she'd know I was joking.

"I'd love to have her. I just needed you to hear you're doing well. It's not easy, you know. Raising a kid alone."

Her words hung in the air a moment, two.

"I—" *I, what?* Well, I never got the words out because Hazel Kane leaned forward, both hands still clutching her basket, and planted a kiss at the corner of my lips. She began to pull away, then evidently changed her mind, and slid sideways to get me full on the mouth. I buried my surprise and kissed her back, hoping I still remembered how this shit was supposed to work. A small giggle told me I was either doing good—excuse me, well—or real bad.

The kiss lasted a handful of seconds or hours. One or the other, for sure. When it broke off, she stepped back with fire-red cheeks and a smile that poked at her earlobes.

"Thanks," I said. The latest in a long line of dumb things that shot out my mouth when Hazel was around. "For dinner," I added. "Thank you for dinner. I had a nice time, which I already said, but I figure I might as well mention it again while you're still here. I think I'd like to do it again. The food, I mean. Not the other part, the part that just happened, not that I—"

Hazel's smile dropped, the corners pulled into a frown and cut my ramble off at the knees.

"What?" I asked. "What's wrong?"

"You don't smell that?"

First the rambling nonsense, then a nasty smell. My first contact with a woman in some time, and I guess my last.

Then I caught a whiff. A reek like dried-up riverbed and dead animal stung my nostrils, threatening to haul those coriander potatoes up by the bootstraps and spill them all over the sand. "Yeah, I got it now. I'm sorry. I don't know what—"

Hazel screamed, and the night seemed to part around it. So loud, they must've heard it back in the town proper. She grabbed at my shoulders and tried to hide behind me. I reached for my revolver only to remember I wasn't wearing it, then spun to see a figure watching from the open desert. Far enough away to cloud my judgment. It had to be. Because otherwise, the fucking thing was over seven feet tall.

It lumbered closer, and clouded judgment be damned, it might've been closer to eight feet.

"Get inside," I whispered. "Tell Alice to fetch my gun, then you hide under a bed or something, hear me?"

Hazel kept quiet and still, all except for her claws digging into me.

"Go," I said, and stepped forward, breaking the trance. Hazel dashed inside, shutting the door as quietly as you could expect from a person in such a panic.

A cloud of breath twirled up toward the moon as I shouted into the darkness. "If you're just passing by, my friend, we ain't got no problem. Though I'd prefer you gave my place a bit of a wider berth. Land's wide open. Plenty of room for everybody."

The figure stumbled forward another couple of steps.

A drunk, I thought. *And it had to be one that outweighed most cattle.*

I kept quiet, listening for the click of the door, or better yet, the click of a rifle. Suddenly, that fear caught up with me. Here I was, unarmed, little more than a few lunges away from this massive, stinky gentleman, and the help I'd sent was likely lying in a stupor on the parlor floor.

"Last warning before I grab my gun, buddy. I don't much care for you scaring my kid and my ... Well, just find another way to get home."

Just turn, I begged silently, *wander off into that great dark.* Instead, he ran full on ahead, straight at me.

As soon as the moonlight hit his face, realization dawned. I'd never met the giant before, but I knew him all the same.

CHAPTER 12

MOGEY

Henry Taff liked to tell stories. And he was good at it. So good, in fact, that his rapt listeners had trouble deciding the difference between fact and bullshit. Between "I heard" and "I know."

Truth be told, it was the best way he could've settled a young kid named Rory Daggett into his new home after said kid had watched the tops of his parents' heads get blown out a train car window.

The mark of any great storyteller is the ability to read his audience and adjust on the fly. Henry could control the smile on his wife's face—Willie, my adoptive mom—like it was attached to a dial. Turn it down at the sad parts, crank it all the way up at the happy endings, and split it with bursts of laughter just when it appeared she might get up to start supper or sweep the entryway. Of course, he knew how to do it, he'd had years and years of practice.

With me, it was walking a tightrope. Do you tell a sad story to a kid who's experienced tragedy? A scary story to someone who's survived real horrors? Something brimming with joy to a listener who understands the world isn't really like that?

It was a mystery, and yet, he approached it like a puzzle he meant to solve.

As it turned out, I loved a good monster story. A nice balance of all three tightrope emotions. Because a monster isn't all that scary if the tragedy unfolds just outside the edges of the story. That takes care of your sad. The happy? Well, when you're telling a monster story to an eight-year-old, the hero usually wins. It's a hard-fought battle, but somewhat predictable. And then there's your scary, and this is the toughest part to balance. It's got to feel distant. Like it could happen to others, just not to you.

That's why my favorite story took place around a set of mountains, just not the Blackjacks.

Henry'd work up to it by describing the Mogollon mountains, more green and a little taller than the ones around us, and considerably more expansive. They ran through a pretty lengthy portion of the Arizona territory and were home to the Mogollon tribe of natives. More than a few of the natives met their end at the hands of settlers making their way west and being less than willing to share the land.

That's how the story started. Henry went on to mention that the Mogollon tribe fought back to keep their way of life, capturing and sometimes executing the white folks stumbling westward. Three such gentlemen wound up caught and tied to logs. The Mogollon chief ordered the men thrown into the river and his warriors obliged. One of the men drowned when the log flipped over and held him beneath the water. Another cracked and smashed into every rock the fast-moving section of river had to offer and dashed his skull to bits. The third man experienced the best of both worlds. Sometimes Henry left him nameless, other times he called the fella Gideon. So Gideon smacked his head on each passing rock, their sharp edges tearing at his clothes and his skin until the only things covering his shame were blood and rope. Of course, the blood washed off every time the log flipped over, pinning good old Gideon beneath the rushing water until his lungs threatened to burst. Then, through some kind of divine intervention, the log would turn just long enough for Gideon to steal a breath and knock his skull against a rock before he went under again.

Sometimes the story pulled him miles along the river, sometimes days. Always, it took him far from the Mogollon tribe and right to the edge of insanity. Finally, one of the rocks sliced through rope instead of skin and granted Gideon his freedom.

Physically, at least. Because the near-death experience cost him his mind and his humanity. The Mogollon tribe neglected to follow him downriver, and that was alright because once he crawled out of the water, he dragged himself into the nearest cave and nursed his wounds. Depending on Henry's mood, sometimes Gideon dragged the corpses of his compadres into the cave, and well, if I could figure out the implication at ten years old, so can you.

Skip a little bit ahead and Gideon healed up, just not quite right. All those broken bones stretched out his arms and legs, made him gangly and tall. His red hair grew out, streaked with gray, covering not just his head but his entire body. His eyes sunk back into his skull, making him look like an animal, and he fucking stank, like rotted fish and death. At night, he hunted, a lot of times with a weapon hanging by his side, a big old nasty piece of downed tree fashioned into a club. And he wasn't picky. He'd knock the hell out of a cougar and strip the meat from its bones, gather up the corn from a farmer's field under cover of darkness, or maybe break straight for the farmer and drag them kicking and screaming back to his cave.

Anyways, folks started to talk about old Gideon, except by then, nobody knew his name. They just called him the Mogollon monster.

Except for me, I always thought of him as "Mogey" because it made him less scary.

Swathes of reddish-brown hair, caked and crusted together with lord-knows-what, swung in the moonlight as Mogey bolted forward in one hell of a hurry. Those patches of fur were the only thing covering the man—though I couldn't help thinking of him as a creature. They did their job well, revealing a gray, mottled face while leaving the rest of him looking like he'd skinned some great beast and put on its hide as a coat. His sunken, bloodshot eyes set on me as he closed the distance between us, an ugly piece of lumber swinging from his right hand.

And there's the club, I thought.

As he closed the last of the gap between us, he raised the club over his head and brought it down in a swing powerful enough that my head would've been halfway to Mexico if I hadn't rolled out of the way.

"Pip!" I screamed, and dove again to avoid another swing of that massive club. The second scamper brought me right by Mogey's legs and within smelling distance. An unpleasant prospect, only I had bigger concerns. I aimed a kick at his knee, hoping for some give and a crunch. All I got was a vibration like a plucked fiddle string running up my own leg. The monster screamed, and it sounded eerily like a woman.

"The gun, Pip! If you can hear me, for Christ's sake, take a shot!"

With a grunt, he swung the club, burying it in the sand only inches from my leg. The chunk of wood stuck fast, and I saw an opportunity. Wrapping my hands around the grip, I kicked off and swung around, driving both boots into a hairy set of ribs. It was like striking a cottonwood tree and it sent me sprawling backward. When I hit the ground, I crawled away and struggled to my feet, arms up to protect my head.

Mogey tore his club free from the sand and swayed, watching me. He looked like a wolf, lurking in the tall grass, trying to decide whether this particular meal was worth the trouble. I'd never seen the kind of ape they had in Africa, but I'd seen drawings, and that was the closest comparison I could make. The Mogollon monster was human in stature and shape. Animal in every other regard. When Henry told the story, I always pictured a wild man. Still a man, though. If any of that was true, and not just Henry spinning yarns, then there was no Gideon left in this thing.

Mogey seemed to size me up even as I did the same to him, staring through me with those bestial eyes, buried in folds of pallid gray skin. Then he hauled back and chucked his club at me. Maybe it was the fact that he appeared like a stupid animal that took me by surprise, but it smacked into my chest before I even knew what was happening. I fell backward, a pounding ache taking hold of my sternum before I hit the sand. A sharp pain stabbed at my lungs and when I tried to suck in a breath, only a shallow wheeze escaped.

Panic seized me in its grip as I desperately tried to draw breath, failing again and again. I rolled in the sand, trying to pick a direction and stick to it, maybe outcrawl the mammoth creature that had just immobilized its prey.

Another hitched breath, like there was something stuck in my throat. The first footfall shook the earth as I writhed in the dirt, clutching my chest, waiting for my breath to turn back on or for the big beastie to squash my head and put me out of my misery. What an embarrassing way to go.

That dead-fish stink clawed at my nose, acting as the first hint that maybe my breathing was about to get its gears moving once more. Another footstep rattled a thousand grains of sand. If Mogey kept stomping like this, he might just vibrate me home and we could forget about this unfortunate little run-in. Another thundering boom. The footsteps sounded far enough apart to tell me the monster was in no hurry. Was he toying with his food or just being cautious because I kept kicking him?

Didn't really matter one way or the other, because his face appeared overhead, blocking out the moon. A few trickles of breath had started sneaking back in. Enough that I knew I wasn't going to die from my injury. Just not enough air to yell for Alice.

My heart hurt a bit at the thought. Since the day I'd found her starving away in the upstairs room of my parents' home, we'd watched each other's backs. *You're all I have*, she'd signed to me when we were on the lam, and I'd signed it back, and we made sure to remind each other regularly. Now here I was, about to be eaten by a story come to life, and she was nowhere to be found.

Mogey leaned down, baring black-spotted teeth, dripping strings of saliva that fell to coat my shirt. Enough spittle you could hear the *plinkity-plonk* of each drop as it struck, even over the sound of the beast's low growl. He moved slow enough that I had time to study his teeth, larger than average for sure, devoid of the pointy canines you typically saw in those ape drawings, so maybe this fucker was human after all.

Snarling, the monster knelt on me, pressing an immense weight on my chest. Those sneaking breaths became stolen hints of air. For a moment, it wasn't even enough to smell the stink coming off the thing any longer. Then he leaned in and blew a gust of hot, rank breath on me, close enough to spot brownish-green chunks of meat jammed between his worn and ragged teeth. Whether because that was the color of what he ate or the remnants had festered in there long enough to change hue, I couldn't guess. Nor did I want to. The teeth were powerful enough to rip my throat out, just not sharp enough to make it quick. I grunted out some hapless combination of "Help," "Stop," and "Get off me." A slop of words that made the creature cock his head to the side as he drew closer.

Arms pinned by my side, I did the only thing I could, prayed and pissed a little while I watched the teeth come closer and waited for the pain to hit. Then a stealthy *crack*.

My skull, surely, or my ribcage giving out under the thing's weight. Or maybe that's just the sound death made when you experienced it instead of delivering it. I waited for the pain to hit, for as long as I could hold my breath, and when no fresh agony flooded my chest, I realized I knew the sound of that echoing crack. A rifle shot.

Mogey didn't go flying off me, so I had to assume the shot had done nothing except distract him. I seized the opportunity and yanked my arms free, reached up and jabbed my thumbs into the creature's eyes. He unleashed another one of those high-pitched, ladylike screams and scrambled backward off me.

"Rory!" called a voice, raw and desperate.

Hazel, must be, and I'd see to her needs after. For the moment, I had some luck to press. I felt along the ground for anything I could use, eventually winding up with a fist-sized rock, then I sucked in the biggest breath my half-working lungs could handle, climbed to my feet and swung all in one motion. With as much power behind it as I could muster, the stone sliced open a gash on the monster's forehead and sent his beady little eyes rolling back in his skull. He fell backward, and I climbed on top of him and held the rock over my head, our positions reversed from only a moment ago.

When his eyes quit twirling and rested on me, I could almost believe a man used to live behind them, even if he was long gone. The Mogollon monster was nothing but an animal now, one that seemed mighty scared. I held the rock aloft as I pictured the stars in Ghost's eyes; the chimera trying to light me up like a campfire, not because it was mean, but because I'd interrupted its meal, scared it. I imagined those goat-sucker dogs and the way they looked when one of their own had gone down at the behest of a bullet. And I decided enough animals had bled out in the Buzzard's Edge sand just lately.

After all, we were song dogs ourselves. And as strange a place as this town could be, at some point you had to send coincidence packing and embrace conspiracy.

Holding the rock high, I stood and yelled at the mangy thing. Mogey somehow appeared both larger than any man and smaller than a child. "Go on," I shouted. "Git!"

And wonder of wonders, he did. Squealing and scampering off into the night. For half a heartbeat, I worried about him coming back with a grudge. Then I remembered that was a human problem.

I let the rock fall and turned toward the house. There stood Hazel, clutching a rifle like it might try to bite if she loosened her grip. A plume of smoke drifted off the end and things made more, if not total, sense.

She missed. Alice wouldn't have.

That's when I noticed Hazel shaking. Her wide-eyed face looked bloodless. She tilted her head toward the front door.

"You've gotta come in," she said. "I think something's wrong with Alice."

Chapter 13

The Best We Can Do

As a parent, a protector, you never want to hear those words about your own kid. Your heart races and your normally logical head jumps to the worst conclusions. All the same, I had a pretty good idea about what was going on with Alice.

When Hazel led me inside, Alice's appearance confirmed my guess. I found her flat on the bed, arms and legs spread-eagle. Sweat doused her pale face, and her eyes darted back and forth, staring through the ceiling like she was reading a book writ upon the moon.

"Pip," I whispered as I crossed the room.

Hazel shot me a strange look and remained by the doorway.

I went to take my hat off, only to find I wasn't wearing one, and knelt by the bed. "Pip's what I used to call her before she ever told me her name. I guess it kinda stuck."

"Is she alright?"

"She will be," I said, and I tried real hard to believe myself. "It's happened before." I let a beat pass and decided to bring Hazel in. "It was before you moved here, but you ever hear about the Devil's Cavern massacre?"

"Of course," she said, then shrugged, appearing to almost reconsider. "Some, anyway. The whole town marched north and went to war with itself. A lot of people didn't make it back. I … I guess never thought too hard about the why."

"Short version is a woman named Mary McHugh took over as sheriff with something of a vendetta against the town." *Against me*, I thought. "If you only believe in the natural world, the things you can see, hear, smell, and touch yourself, then the next part is a hard sell. If you've seen things you can't quite explain, like a giant monster beating your host half to death, then I guess you could buy what happened at Devil's Cavern."

Alice shifted in the bed, the first movement beyond fluttering eyes since I'd walked in the room. I squeezed her hand and waited for Hazel to weigh in. She didn't.

"Alice got gutshot by McHugh. For a moment, it sure looked like the world was coming to an end. At least that's the way I took it." I wet my lips. "Funny. I guess I haven't thought much about it since. Almost lost my little girl that day and I just sorta … went on. What a fucked-up thing to do, huh?"

I didn't leave her time to answer. What would I have even expected her to say?

"McHugh had this … well, let's call it a healing pool. Odd thing and I won't pretend to know how it worked, but Pip's here in the land of the living, so clearly it did. And it saved her life, a moment or two before the cavern roof caved in. Thad Locke helped me ferry her to safety and I guess I'll always owe him for that. Thing is, when she came around, that bullet hole had disappeared and besides what you're seeing now, there were never any complications." I chuckled. "Of course, this is one big motherfucker of a complication. Excuse my language, Miss Kane. Not very gentlemanly of me."

Hazel nodded, arms crossed, hair sticking up in a few new directions. At some point, she'd dropped the rifle, left it somewhere out of sight.

"When Alice woke up," I said, "she saw flashes of things that were going to happen, and I'm starting to think they always revolve around someone's death. It's happened twice before. The first time, she saw a fire taking out the cooperage and trapping one man inside, a man who just so happened to be the former mayor's brother. Strange old world, isn't it?"

She agreed that it was.

"Second time was a little closer to the moment of impact. A few days ago, when those dog creatures tore through the town, she saw that coming too. Just about too late to warn us, although she did show up with her iron, and that surely was a great help. She can see death before it happens, Hazel. Vague images, rarely definitive and not always obvious. Then there's the lead time beforehand. It's a small sample size, but sometimes it's weeks, sometimes hours." Alice blinked rapidly, and I caught the hint of a pupil wrapped in frozen-lake blue. "Which will it be this time, I wonder," I said softly, mostly to myself.

"It's a terrible burden for a child." Hazel stepped forward and rested a hand on my shoulder.

"Yes, it is. Sometimes I wonder if I put too much on her. She's tough as nails. Never doubt that. But I've brought her along on errands no kid her age should be asked to join. She always came willingly, and even though I'd put her in danger, I don't believe she'd have it any other way. Still, that question rests in your mind. What could I have done differently? Did I do the right thing?"

I looked up toward Hazel like she might have an answer, then shrugged.

"Then something like this second sight comes along. And like you say, it's a terrible burden, and I put her in the position to receive it. Now that she's got it?" I shook my head and lowered it to stare at the floor. "There's nothing I can do to relieve her of it."

Hazel laid her other hand on my opposite shoulder. A warmth spread through my body that I didn't realize I'd been missing. "Sometimes," she said, "the best we can do is the best we can do."

"Yeah?"

"When I found her," said Hazel, "she was signing. I recognized some, but …" She shook her head. "She made the sign for 'walk.' Two hands palm down, waving back and forth in unison, right? Then pointed toward her feet."

"Walk down," I said. "That doesn't mean anything to me. Go on."

"I didn't know the next ones. She—" Hazel touched her fingers to her chest, holding them in place while she brought her knuckles close together. "She did this, then made the sign for 'eyes'."

"Animal eyes," I said. "Huh. Was that it?"

She shook her head and raised her right hand, pointer finger up, then twirled it around. "That, then the number one."

"That's the sign for 'alone.' I don't know, maybe the 'one' is just doubling down. One person all on their lonesome when they—" I cleared my throat. "Walk, down, animal eyes, and alone. Lordy, Hazel, this is the strangest set yet."

That's when Alice squeezed my hand back. I lifted my head to find her watching me, clear-eyed.

"What'd you see, Pip?"

As if the first clues weren't odd enough, she added another. She held both hands up to her throat and my heart almost broke as I took in the fear in her face.

"Does that mean what I think it does?" asked Hazel.

Locke showed up early the next morning wearing a frown that could've frightened a scorpion back into its burrow. The kind of look that didn't appear too receptive to hearing about Alice's fit the night before. Not that it would've done much good, anyway. Once she came to, it became clear the pictures that lit up her head were murky at best.

Turned out "walk down" went together, but if there was more, Alice had gone foggy on it. There was a lone figure choking to death, sure, but who might that lone figure be?

Before I could decide what to tell him about Alice, he held up a hand and started rattling.

"Yesterday, I felt it inappropriate to goad you into declaring a mayoral run, but something's happened, and I must ask you, both as a transplanted resident of this town, and a … a friend, to make up your mind. And Rory, I understand you do not wish to commit yourself to such an office. Still, I must urge you to strongly consider."

"Good morning to you, too, sunshine. You want to tell me what's happened and why it's up to me to fix it?"

"Mr. Farrell has left the comforts of the Scarlet Revolver," said Locke.

"I know I'm just a lowly deputy, Thad, but I'm pretty sure he's allowed to do that."

"Listen, goddammit, and stop making everything into a joke." Anger flashed in his eyes. Real bright-red anger. It flamed for a second, then vanished to nothing. Not calm. The last time I'd seen that look in his eyes was after he'd dragged a knife across some shithead's throat back at Devil's Cavern.

"Alright," I said, cowed and a little taken aback. "I'm listening."

Locke blinked, and when he opened his eyes, the light was back. "As I said, Mr. Farrell has made his way among the people. He is shaking hands and making promises. One such promise is that the town under his watch will not require the vigilante justice of one Rory Daggett. Another, significantly more troubling announcement, was that the election will take place tomorrow."

"But you haven't—"

Locke fixed me with a look that filled in the blanks.

"It is a savvy move. Farrell realizes that the more time that passes, the more likely opposition will arise. Enough time has elapsed that no one can claim fair opportunity was not given. It is also cunning because of the bind it puts me in."

"I'll say."

Locke let the ghost of a smirk shine through, and I could almost forget the menace he'd affected only moments ago. "It is within my power to contradict him publicly, but I cannot do so without making the office of sheriff look foolish, and as though it has lost all control of goings on. Farrell has already threatened to take my position. If the townspeople rally behind him, it will be nearly impossible for him to make any other decision." He stared off at the sun, like he'd only just realized the hour. "To tell the truth, I'm not sure how much additional time would even benefit our case. Therefore, your candidacy. It must be now or never."

He didn't need to say that "never" would be as good as handing Alexander Farrell the reins.

I pinched the bridge of my nose, and thought of Alice, Hazel, even Nola. All the chances I'd had to talk this through with each one, and the way I'd brushed it under the carpet and pretended it wasn't happening. I couldn't wait for the ire of three women to fall upon me for making a decision on my lonesome.

"Let's say, I'm in. What do I gotta do?"

"Excellent. There—"

"Whoa there. I didn't say yes. I'm saying maybe. Not no."

The look that took over his face echoed the voice in my head. *You did say yes, Daggett. Just not out loud.*

"There will be paperwork, which I should be happy to guide you through. The best course of action would be to make our way to town immediately and announce your entrance into the race. And of course, your platform."

"My what?"

"Your ideas," said Locke.

"Fantastic. While we walk, would you mind telling me what those are?"

CHAPTER 14

WOLVES DRESSED LIKE SHEEP

Five minutes.

Five minutes and we were on our way. All I had to do was ask Thad to kindly wait outside while I snuck into Alice's room and woke the sleeping girls. No funny stuff. Just that after being attacked by a giant ape-man, I hadn't felt great about sending Hazel walking home alone in the dark. Of course, a gentleman would've walked her home, but Alice's state from the night before snuffed out the coals on that idea.

What could I do besides make sure Alice had her six-shooter close by and leave the two of them to get some rest while I paced the parlor like a big bag of nerves until the sun started poking at the window blinds?

Yeah, exactly.

So, I gave them a nudge, told them I was off to town, and would be back in a bit. They should get some rest and hang around the homestead for a bit. Hazel looked at me with a hint of protest, then seemed to remember it was Saturday. Probably one of the main reasons she suggested our get-together for the previous night. See, I can cast doubt on character too.

Eyes half shut, Alice jutted out her thumb like she was cocking an invisible revolver hammer and curled her pointer finger to pull the trigger. She flung that hand forward. When she brought it back to her chin, she had her pointer and thumb locked in a circle.

"I'll be back before you know it," I said.

Any other day, Locke and I would've dwelled on the Mogollon monster a bit longer. Not being from the area, he'd never heard of it. Though the description reminded him of something called a skunk ape from his time spent down Alabama way. I thought it a pretty dead-on name for such a creature.

Instead, our time crunching through the wild sands between home and the Buzzard's Edge line was spent talking about promises to be made. And I even understood the majority. Not bad for a morning's work.

When we entered town, I pulled my hat low, afraid of getting chased through the streets again. Except the attention appeared turned in a different direction. Nope, Alexander Farrell was hardly all that difficult to find. He stood in front of the sheriff's office, clutching the rail like a podium and speaking to a gathered mass of townsfolk. Out there in the sunlight, he struck an imposing image, looming a couple inches above the nearest people, and not just because he was planted on a porch. He wore all black, except for a cow-skull-white shirt beneath his suit jacket, half-hidden beneath a waistcoat. At first glance, that waistcoat seemed to be using all its strength to hold back the man's gut, but watching him there, and remembering the way he'd emerged from the naked fella's room without a drop of blood on him, I wondered if he was really as soft as he wanted people to think. Even from a distance, you could hear his voice, all at once booming and as smooth as the suit material that looked like it cost a pretty penny.

"Moses Harvey frequented my establishment, kept quarters on the top floor. I won't deny that," he said. "A ravening wolf in sheep's clothing, as the good book does say. It sickens me that he made his plans under my own roof, but that does not change the fact that they were his plans. Had I only known he would sink so low as to threaten the life of a child, to start a fire with intent to murder, all for some ill-conceived plot of revenge, I would never have opened my doors to him."

Here he paused and took a moment to lock eyes with as many folks in the crowd as dared to meet his own. "Some of you might say—and you would be perfectly within your right—that this oversight should disqualify me from public trust. To those few, I would not make excuses. I would simply say my eyes have been opened to what deceit can look like. Call it contrition, call it what you like, but my candidacy for mayor of Buzzard's Edge represents not more of the same: abuse of power, greed, lust, folks that take the law into their own hands. It represents a commitment to be sober and vigilant. As Peter says, our adversary walks about like a roaring lion seeking whom he might devour. Rarely does the adversary stroll down the middle of the street. He wears many masks, takes many forms, and steals quietly when our backs are turned." He pounded his fist and shook the sturdy wooden railing with each word. "We will not allow this great town to be stolen from under our feet."

Another glance at the crowd. "When you vote tomorrow, remember that there may be no alternative on the ballot, but still, I will strive to earn the vote of every man in Buzzard's Edge."

"Well now, hold on, Mr. Farrell. Because it seems to me that you're not alone on that there ballot." As he'd driven his impassioned pleas into the hearts and minds of the crowd, I'd squeezed through cracks and shimmied my way toward him for a perfectly placed interjection that would've made any watchmaker proud.

As I joined him on the sheriff's porch, taking a place at the other side of the step-up, Farrell drew his face into a great grin. One with a trace of nerves. Only a trace, though. Anyone farther away than me likely wouldn't notice the way his eyes opened a bit too wide, stretching his crow's feet uncomfortably tight.

"Mr. Daggett," he said, his voice slipping easily back into that charming boom. "Rory Daggett, ladies and gentlemen, the hero of Buzzard's Edge. I was not informed of any other applicants running for mayor."

I met his smile and returned him one that I hoped held a little more humor. "Funny thing, Alex. I meant to get around to it. I woke up today and realized that the election was tomorrow." I smacked my forehead. "Figured I better go ahead and get on that."

A few chuckles drifted from the back of the crowd.

"I welcome the challenge," he said, and stepped forward to shake my hand. Nola was right. Snake was a far better comparison than any other animal. He clutched my hand with an iron grip and leaned in. "Good luck," he whispered. "Hero you may be, but you don't know how to win a crowd."

I pulled him close and patted him on the back. "You sent a dragon-lion, a pack of devil dogs, and the goddamn Mogollon monster to take me out, and yet here I stand. Pretty sure I can figure out the crowd part of this."

He didn't so much let go of my hand as drop it and turn the same skull-bleach-white as his shirt. If I'm honest, it knocked me off my guard, because he looked scared, and not the kind of fright you see in a man who's been caught. More the kind you'd expect from a man who's been surprised. I shook it away and turned my attention back to the people.

"Ladies and gents, boys and girls, children of all ages. Mr. Farrell has referred to me as the hero of Buzzard's Edge, and I couldn't hate that any worse. Don't get me wrong, I'm honored by the appreciation, but all I did was help the town sheriff investigate a murder and defend my daughter. I bet any of you would've done the same. Before I let him finish what I'm sure was a very well-rehearsed speech with a bit more fist pounding, let me address the part he's working up in his mind right about now."

I turned and met Farrell's eyes. They'd lost that fear, and he'd gained some color back. He motioned for me to go on.

"First off, he wouldn't be wrong in saying I've got no experience. But that don't mean I plan to kick my feet up and sit around all day sipping whiskey and threatening orphans. If you'll have me, I say we undertake a search for a Marshall to bolster our sheriff's office. Thing is, Mr. Farrell's plea about wolves dressed like sheep isn't bad, but it also ain't a plan."

This was Thad's first idea. Get him some real help without promoting him and sprinkling the sweet flavor of favoritism all over his reputation.

"See, two possible things about Moses Harvey," I went on. "He either turned criminal fast as a rattlesnake when you snag its tail or he always leaned in that direction. Somebody once said to me, 'once a killer, always a killer' and that's stuck with me. That in mind, Mayor Harvey ran this place for quite some time. The next person in charge might find some ugly surprises in the places they got hired to look. So, we bring in a respected townsperson, open to nominations, to sift through the finances and make sure everything's on the level. See, Mr. Farrell's not wrong that I don't know how to mayor. But I tell you what, I'm more than willing to bring in people to help and let you all see how I'm doing it along the way. Honesty is what I'm preaching, no more sheep clothing. Best way to pull that off? Take down the walls and make sure people can see the wolf tiptoeing around. And hey, if that sounds alright to you, consider casting your vote for Rory Daggett tomorrow. Thank you all."

I waved and smiled so big my face started to hurt. It almost felt like I should say more, only the crowd roared so over-the-top loud, they wouldn't have heard it anyway. I turned to Farrell, expecting to see him red and seething, maybe clutching the rail so tight he'd leave the indents of his fingers behind. Instead, he stared out over the crowd, smiling to himself.

Well, I couldn't have that.

Before I descended into the human sea, I ambled over toward Farrell and leaned in. "Well, then, may the best man win tomorrow." His smile twitched. "Oh, and Alex? You ever threaten my daughter again and I'll shoot you dead in the middle of the street and see just how easy it is to win a race with no opposition."

"Careful, boy," was all he said, with a chill to his tone, then he went back to staring.

I gave him a hard nod, set down the single step, and lost myself among the people. A variety of cries rattled off my shoulders.

"Atta boy, Daggett."

"Henry'd be proud."

"Show that gulldarn robber baron."

Some were not so friendly.

"Might want to stay back on the farm, boy. Leave the runnin' of things to them that are grown."

"How you gon' have time to get a job with that little deaf girl hangin' off your arm?"

"Wet nurse!"

I spun to find the last two voices, a snarl growing on my lips, and found only Thad Locke. He wrapped an arm around my shoulder and set me to walking. "Pay them no mind. Some have far too little going on between their ears to speak with poise. You'll never gain their votes, only lose others."

As if Locke had plugged up my ears, the voices became a collective dull ringing. Some, no doubt infused with anger, bounced off and died in the sand.

"Remember, Rory, that there is nothing in the world you can do to make everyone like you. Some simply have hate far too deeply ingrained within their heart. I believe that good recognizes good." He stopped speaking for a moment, simply moved forward in silence and with a thoughtful glint in his eye. "Perhaps the opposite is true, as well. Regardless, know that you were not only the most obvious choice on short notice to put disorder back into some semblance of order, but the right choice is well. There is no man I've met whose heart is more up to the task."

A dozen and a half replies spun through my mind, and maybe they jammed up at the exit, because nothing came out. By then, we'd broken out of the crowd. I turned to take one last glance at the people who would cast their votes the next day. A small wave caught my eye. There stood Miss Nola Betts, leaning half off the porch of her tailor shop. The woman who typically appeared neither pleased nor displeased at least seemed amused for the moment.

I guess that was something. This whole charade might not be advisable or even halfway to smart, but I supposed it would be entertaining.

"You think I'd have to move back into town if I win?" I asked Hazel.

The blaze of daylight made the walk back to her place feel a whole lot safer, while also making it a struggle to believe the showdown with the Mogollon monster the night before had really happened. I might not have bought it at all if not for the scattered patches of dried brown blood back near the homestead. Either the Buzzard's Edge sand hadn't gotten around to drinking its fill, or it didn't like the taste of monster meat. "Like, are you allowed to be in charge if it takes half an hour at a sprint to get to town?"

Hazel smiled and looked down. "Worry about one thing at a time, I'd say. There'll be plenty to fret over in the long term. Always is."

Alice led the way, a good distance ahead of me and Hazel, pretending not to listen in and doing a piss-poor job of it all. Critters scampered over the sand in the dead, dry patch between Casa Daggett and the rest of civilization. As they always did. Much smaller and more fearful than vicious. Wild how they could exist in the same world as Mogey and the devil dogs.

"Thanks for sticking around. Sorry I couldn't give you much of a heads up. Caught me by surprise too. Christ, Hazel. I'm minding my own business in my own home, strange woman passed out in the other room. An hour later, I'm giving a speech to half the town. Not anything I signed up for, that's for sure."

"You might've found yourself with more time for preparation had you listened to me in the first place." There was a lightness to her voice. Melodic without being showy, the alto part of a church hymn. Something to support the main melody, all the while shining. It's just that most folks never pay attention to the alto part.

I was listening.

Stopping short, I kicked up a puff of sand. "Last night," I said, then paused, chewing on my tongue. "I kind of like you, Hazel, and I'm not wild about the turn our first try at courting took near the end. When this all settles down a bit, I'd like to invite you over proper. Maybe I cook for you next time, and we hold off on the creature attacks."

"Rory," she said, and breathed deep. "I'd like that. The only thing is, I do wonder if things ever settle down for you. Even a little bit."

"Guess that depends on how hard we lean on 'little bit'. I s'pose I'd understand if it was all too much."

Up ahead, shoulders slumped, Alice trudged through a patch of withered grass. Never quite one to skip, she used to at least scamper about. Lately, though? Well, I guess I wouldn't be hopping around all jolly if I had the sort of visions she did. Complicated and still somehow too broad to instill confidence.

She was kind enough to pretend not to notice when Hazel leaned in to kiss me. There was something about that second time that made me feel a little whiskey-buzzed. Just a little.

When Hazel pulled away, she smiled to herself and looked down. Alice caught us with a look that sent her eyebrows up toward her hairline. There was more "Are you coming or not?" to her eyes than shock or surprise.

I took Hazel's hand, and we walked the rest of the way to her place in a comfortable quiet.

CHAPTER 15

SINGING WITH NO VOICE

By Thad's insistence—a note slid under the front door if you can believe it—Alice and I stayed at home the rest of the day, and into the next.

My dearest Rory, he wrote.

Though it might seem counterintuitive to disappear from the public eye for a day or two, I daresay it's in your best interest. The girl's, as well. From what I can gather, you made a positive impression on the citizens this morning, and it would be to your advantage to let it linger in their hearts and minds. I confess I worried that Mr. Farrell might conjure up some wicked words, a surprise to us both, and leave you looking the fool—

Thanks, Thad.

—in front of a sizable crowd. Nonetheless, it would not do to give him the opportunity. I must also admit that if your supposition is correct, that Farrell is somehow unleashing these abominable creatures to assault your person, it would be unwise to stroll around town and put people in danger.

I do solemnly swear to be on my guard all the next two days, and should anything develop, I shall send for you immediately. Try to get some rest, and regardless of the outcome, I shall contact you on the morrow.

Most humbly yours,

Thaddeus Locke, Sheriff

So, we waited. A few card games, a little conversation, some leftover potatoes, and two pairs of watchful eyes, glancing over to the window every so often to check on the horizon. The darkness was big, always was this far out in the world, and more than ever, I missed Ghost's soft whinnies and stomping feet echoing out from the back. Nothing appeared to be watching, however. No mangy pack of dogs, no man-beasts, and no fire-breathing cougar monster. Never mind all the shit I'd heard stories about but never laid eyes on. After all, who knew what else Alexander Farrell had up his sleeve?

Long after we'd given up on the cards and dinner was a distant enough memory to find me hungry again, Alice rapped twice on the floor, yanking me back from the thoughts I'd gotten lost in.

"Sorry, Pip, I missed that. Trouble?"

She shook her head, then put a flat hand against her temple like a salute. When she brought it forward, she closed it into a fist, all but her thumb and pinky.

"Why what?"

After a moment of lip-chewing thought, she started spelling. M-A-Y-O-R.

I let the question sit between us, not because I didn't think it deserved an answer, more because I still didn't have one.

Impatiently, she tapped her chest and raised her eyebrows to add a question mark.

Me? Because of me?

"In a way, I guess. Maybe I thought of the fella Locke wanted me to go up against, remembered the unpleasant stuff he said, the way Vivian and Drea looked so scared of him." I lowered my voice. "What he might've done to some of the other girls there. It made the decision quicker, if not different. I don't know, Pip. Truth be told, I don't really want it. It's more like …" I sighed and quietly pleaded for the answers to come running.

H-A-Z-E-L

"No." I chuckled. "I don't know. She seemed alright with saying hello when she thought I was just a volunteer sheriff's deputy. That ain't it. Promise. And I'd tell you if it was."

Frustration collected on that little girl's face. She mashed her fingers into fists, wedging her thumbs between pointer and middle fingers, then snapped the fists outward like she was cracking a whip.

"Alright, alright. How about this? It's like when you had those goat-sucker dogs dead to rights the other day, and you wanted to put 'em down. I could see it in your eyes. You didn't, though."

The wrinkles on her forehead shifted from frustration to confusion. She pointed to me, then chopped her right hand into her left palm.

"I did say stop." I shrugged. "But are you telling me there wasn't a moment where you weighed whether or not to listen?"

Her face smoothed over. No reply.

"You're not some wayward kid, that's not what I'm saying. Just that you showed up on my doorstep—my second floor, anyway—with this sharp notion of right and wrong, and the ability to make those decisions on your own. Way beyond the scope of any other kid your age. Pip, if I thought I'd been aiming you at things and letting you knock 'em dead all this time, that wouldn't make me much of a father. In fact, I'd say it would make me as much a monster as anyone we've stood together against."

She twirled her fingers in a motion you could read without knowing a lick of sign language.

Get to the point, Daggett.

"Sometimes," I said. "you just know right is right, and you don't have to think too hard on it. And sometimes, you make that choice even when you don't want to, hoping you ain't wrong. Hoping it's the best way that lies in front of you to keep more people from getting hurt."

Alice tilted her head, seeming to take it in.

I leaned forward, whispered softly, "I ain't heard about any more dog attacks since you let those mongrels live. You?"

She put on a half-cocked smile. The kind a person wore when their mind was running too fast to commit to sincerity. With a gesture that bordered on carefree, she crooked her index finger and batted it forward. Her eyes let me know it was a question. One that contained worlds.

Do you need to?

I searched her face for any hint of how she meant it. Did it have to be me? Nobody else came to mind. Had I thought it all the way through? We both knew I hadn't, so no sense in lying. Or maybe, wasn't it time to let this place fend for itself?

Surely, somewhere out there, an answer existed for that last question. Just as surely, I wouldn't find it by tomorrow.

"What would we do, kid? I mean, we could pick up and try our luck farther west. Head east back to civilization. I don't know about you, but neither one of those ideas sets my hair on fire." My knee cracked like dry kindling as I stood and my sore calf smarted after sitting still for too long. Christ, I guess I was about the oldest twenty-four-year-old in Buzzard's Edge. "Maybe us song dogs just belong in the desert."

Alice looked up, wide-eyed, tapping the fingers of one hand against the other palm, like she couldn't quite find the words. Finally, she pointed to herself with her right hand, clapped her pointer and middle fingers to her thumb, then shaped a V and scraped up her throat toward her chin.

"I don't have a voice," she had said.

The unsaid part? "So how could I be a song dog?"

"I don't think I've told you much about my mother, Pip. My first mother, the one Noose took from me. She played piano, long before I was born, and taught me how to get around on it when I was little. I haven't played in, well, a long time. Never wanted to after she died. But if I think real hard, I can still hear the graceful way her hands flew over the keys, the tense chords finding their way to the perfect resolution. Somehow her delicate little hands stretched into impossible shapes to draw perfection out of that instrument. And every time she played, she'd clamp her mouth shut so tight it should've cut off her lungs, and she wouldn't ease up until she'd finished the song. Then she'd sit there for a moment, looking tired, before a smile found its way onto her face, and she'd invite me to try my hand."

Alice pointed to herself, then raised her closed right fist, and flicked her pointer finger at the ceiling.

"No," I laughed. "Maybe that was a little dense. So let me put it this way. Not everyone uses their voice to sing, and sometimes people who find a different way have the most to say."

She formed a circle with her thumb and pointer, then brought the shape from her chest forward, along with a tired smile. "I like that," was how I understood it.

"Come on," I said, helping her to her feet. "Big day tomorrow. Let's try and get some sleep."

For the second night in a row, sleep proved hard to find, and near impossible to hold onto. I snuck a few winks here and there. Every time I opened my eyes, though, it was just as dark outside. Alice's soft, steady breaths drifted in from the next room, a comfort even with my nerves on edge. One of those nod-outs must have lasted slightly longer than the others because eventually, slivers of light outlined the curtains.

What better way to keep a man's mind from wandering than morning chores?

I started out toward the stable, taking a moment to kneel by the little cross we'd fashioned for Ghost and share a few silent memories. Our lone goat, Clyde, gave me a funny slant-eyed look when I walked in to tidy up. Admittedly, I hadn't spent much time in there since Ghost's death. Clyde stared a moment, then fucked off back to chewing on a piece of wood and smelling like he might be dead. Maybe an hour later, the stable was the cleanest it had been since we built it. Eggs needed collecting, and the hens needed some feed, but as I walked out toward the coop, a spot where fence met gate caught my eye. One I'd been meaning to fix since monsoon season.

No big job, it's just there's always something that seems more immediate. I remembered the day it happened. Ghost trotting around the yard, throwing her head over her shoulder in this grand "Are you looking at me?" gesture until her clumsy ass stumbled straight into the gate. The horse was fine, if a little embarrassed. As embarrassed as a horse can be, anyway.

The hinges fared less well. I figured I could salvage them. As I was sizing up the job, I felt a pair of eyes watching me.

"How about I gather the wood, Pip? You grab the hammer and nails. That's all it should take."

We toiled away as the day went from warm to hot to somewhere just south of hell. I admit we took our time with the job, wanting to make the work last, and keep our hands and minds from wandering too far. It kept conversation at bay, as well. After a night spent piddling around, I didn't have any more clarity on Alice's thoughts and questions. I figured she knew as much.

By the time Alice and me fixed that gate sturdy as a stone, maybe stronger than it had been originally, the sun had left its overhead watchpoint far behind. I clapped the dust from my hands. Alice did the same with a near-silent laugh.

"You've been busy." Thad Locke peered over the other side of the gate, silent and still, like he'd been perched, waiting for the right moment to drop his foot in the mud puddle. His face carried bad news. An ugly omen in and of itself, because Thad's face never carried much of anything.

"There's been another attack," he said, softly. "Two dead this time. Seamus Malone and his wife, Clara."

Both our gazes slipped toward Alice. I dropped mine as quickly as I'd let it wander, hoping she hadn't noticed.

Under. Animal eyes. Alone. Choke.

"What happened?"

"I … First and foremost, I should tell you, I am merely repeating what I've been told. Though I examined the bodies, I did not witness the attack."

"Spill it, Thad."

"A great bird, reddish-brown as clay, and most troubling of all, the size of a man, according to William Malone."

"Jesus, he's what? Five? He saw it kill his parents?"

Pressing on, Thad said, "He hid under the wagon and covered his mouth to keep quiet. The bird made a terrible shrieking noise. William said it was screaming like it was the one being attacked."

"Can't say I've ever seen anything like that around here."

"Nor have I, and Rory, according to William, the bird possessed but one large eye and a razor-sharp break, which it used to pierce the necks of Seamus and Clara, and … drink their blood."

I imagine I must've looked like I'd been drained of blood at that moment.

"That last part, I can confirm," he said.

I shook my head. "Farrell. It's gotta be. What do we do? We've got to put off the election at the very least. Track down the bird, maybe—"

Thad put a hand on my shoulder and clenched his jaw, tightened his lips. "I thought you deserved to be informed about the attack, but it's not the reason I came out."

I watched him for a moment to see if I'd imagined that look, or if he might try to cover it up. His eyes told me everything I needed to know.

"We lost," I said, a thin disbelief in my voice.

Chapter 16

The Path to Carelessness

Agatha stood behind the small counter, looking about as imposing as a ninety-pound elderly woman could hope to pull off. With something dangerously close to a smirk on her face, she blocked the entrance to the Scarlet Revolver.

"He isn't here," she said.

"He isn't here, or he won't see me?" I asked.

She shrugged. "It all comes to the same."

"What if I told you I just wanted to come in for a drink?" I let what I hoped was an endearing smile form on my face.

"Then I'd have to tell you you're as full of shit as a mule and less than half as charming. Kindly take off, Mr. Daggett, before I'm forced to call Lou out here. This time of day? He gets a little bored and becomes partial to snapping a bone or two."

I remembered Lou the bartender from our last trip, and suspected I could leave him bleeding in the dust if it came to it. To what end, though? It seemed there were at least a few regulars in there any time of day. The glares they'd sent us packing with last time made me feel less than welcome. I guess any of them would embrace the chance to help old Lou bend my arm backward. And if that failed, there was still the Pinkerton guard out front with the rifle.

"I didn't mean to be no trouble, Miss Agatha. Kindly tell Mr. Farrell I stopped by to … congratulate him on his win."

"Mayor Farrell," she said.

"Pardon?"

"You said 'Mr. Farrell.' Might not be a bad idea to get your tongue used to saying 'Mayor Farrell' from here on out." That hint of a grin stumbled across her face again. Even with a spark of humor, misery still seeped through.

"I'll try to practice every night before bed, ma'am. You have a lovely day, now."

"He's hiding something," I said, swallowing a piping hot sip of yaupon tea.

"Of course he's hiding something," said Nola. "That's what snakes do."

Clopping the cup down on the counter, I put my head in my hands. "This is stupid. Two days ago, I didn't even want to be mayor. I should be relieved, right?"

Alice ducked out of the back room, clutching her own cup of tea. She slid it next to mine and hopped up on a stool. If Nola Betts wasn't careful, this place was going to turn into a saloon to compete with the Scarlet Revolver.

"You brew this, Pip? It's not bad." I chuckled.

Nola smiled. "She was very helpful while you were out. Even stitched up a pair of pants quick as you like. Telling you, Daggett, I'd say she's got a knack for the work, but I don't half wonder if she'd simply be good at anything she put that mind to."

Alice brought her left arm up to her right shoulder and held it in place while she slid her right hand down it, pointer and pinky held up like bull horns.

Nola's eyebrows jumped. "What's she saying?"

I laughed again, and it almost sounded genuine. "Alice thinks Farrell cheated to win the race. I have yet to tell her she's wrong, just that we might have a tough time proving it."

"Hm, right on all counts, I'd say. Interesting." Nola's gaze wandered toward the ceiling, lingered for a moment or two. "What's stopping you from proving it?" she asked at last.

"Well, doubt, for one. That crowd was welcoming enough, but they didn't seem to hate him. What was that you said about wool over eyes?"

She chuckled to herself.

"Doubt and proof." I sighed. "It fits. You're both right, and Thad wouldn't respond to the accusation. He's trying to keep his professional face on, I suppose, but I worry. I know Thad pretty well and any time he doesn't have a lot to say, it says a lot."

"And here we are having this shindig without him," said Nola. As she continued, she took a small box out from underneath the counter and began rolling a cigarette from its contents. "Where is the illustrious Mr. Locke himself, and why didn't he stop you marching off to the Scarlet Revolver, now that I think about it? That seems like just the type of thing that'd make him grab your arm and waggle a finger in your face, Rory."

As much as I enjoyed Nola's dry wit, I'd had enough laughter for the moment. "When you're right, you're right," I said. "So what old Thad don't know, well, it can't hurt him." I pressed a finger to my lips. "He's, uh, down at the sheriff's office with a couple volunteers, bless him. I don't know how long he waited at the edge of our fence before he finally wore down the gumption to speak up, but he couldn't believe the town could celebrate the hero of Buzzard's Edge one day, then dump me so quickly and unceremoniously. Under the guise of wanting to double check the numbers before making an announcement, but ..." I shrugged and took another sip. "One more piece of evidence in favor of Locke believing Farrell a cheat, I guess."

Alice held her hands up like a pair of spectacles and leaned them forward.

I translated for Nola. "She says it was all for nothing. Yeah, Pip?"

A look of disappointment settled on Alice's face as she nodded.

"Now that just ain't true," said Nola. "Because your daddy and Mr. Locke have the bastard in their crosshairs." She looked at me. "You know he's up to something, just don't know what. Not yet. So, we watch him like a vulture cruising 'round, eyeing up his next meal."

"We, huh?"

Nola finished rolling her cigarette, licked the edges and sealed it tight, then rested it in the corner of her mouth. "Oh, I'm invested, Daggett. On top of all that, I've got years of experience keeping my ear to the ground. I'd like to say I know what Farrell'l do, even before he does, but ... well, here we are." She dug around in the box for a match and struck it on the countertop before touching it to the cigarette and drawing in deeply. A sweet smell filled the air. "Maybe I'm thinking a little too big for my britches, but if you're, shall we say, amenable to the idea of keeping tabs on Farrell, seems to me you could do worse than try to take a peek around his office. If he's careless enough to leave something like that silver coin around, an item that links him to an attempt on your life, well, there's bound to be more."

"I don't know, Miss Betts." I rubbed at the back of my neck.

"It's Nola to you, and you know it."

Alice unleashed one of her silent chuckles, and Nola beamed at her. "I tell you I love this kid?"

"Everything you told me about the man and just the position he's worked himself up into speaks of somebody careful—"

"And I'm certain he started out that way. Fortunately for us, success eventually breeds arrogance, and arrogance points right down the path to carelessness. That's the path that maybe, just maybe, opens those doors."

"I'm not saying it's not worth looking, just wondering if the potential reward is worth trying to get through all the bullshit standing between the street and the office itself. The barman and me have a love-hate thing that mostly focuses on the hate, the lady who runs the front is a stone-cold bitch, and there's even a hired guard standing watch at the front door, one that Thad says wasn't there a week ago. Not to mention, I hear it's a rare occasion that Farrell even leaves the Scarlet Revolver."

Nola studied me a moment, smoke trailing from the end of her cigarette to halo her head. "Rory Daggett," she said. "I won't pretend to understand you inside and out, boy, but my goodness gracious, if you put all those excuses in a wagon, you'd need three horses to pull it." Turning to Alice, she added, "He always this quick to show the white feather?"

Alice put her palms face out and shoved them forward.

Pointing with the cherry of her cigarette, Nola said, "That I understood. He just needs a push, right?"

Alice nodded with a grin that practically split her face.

"Any ideas?" asked Nola.

"We could start by not talking about him like he's not in the room," I added with a frown.

"Where's the fun in that?" asked Nola. Her eyes brightened. "Think I've got one part solved."

I held out a hand, gesturing for her to go on.

"Alright," she said. "How confident are you that Mr. Locke will arrive at the same count this time around?"

Letting my eyes roll back, I tilted my head and said, "Reasonably. If Farrell did find a way to fix the outcome, I can't imagine it was as simple as hoping Thad would count wrong."

"So, he's won then. No way around it. Which means there'd have to be a swearing-in and here's you two, thick as thieves with the sheriff, the gentleman I figure to be in charge of setting the time and place, not to mention running the whole ho-down." She raised her eyebrows as if to say, "You get it?"

I did. And it made me wonder a lot of things, least of all, how a tailor in Buzzard's Edge came to be so damn clever and conniving.

"A swearing-in ceremony, I'd guess. Maybe not all that long, but if there were to be some kind of festivity after, well, that'd buy us some time."

"Now those gears are turning," said Nola.

Alice leaned forward on the counter, like a cougar ready to pounce.

"Okay, it's good, I admit," I said, "But he's not going to close up shop, or drag all his workers down to a ceremony like that. There's no sneaking in that front door, past the matron and all the other folks who probably wouldn't mind digging me a shallow desert grave."

Alice continued staring straight ahead, then without warning, all but sprung out of her chair. The moment she landed, she started spelling with her hands, in such a frenzy that Nola appeared worried and I missed half the letters.

"Love the spirit, Pip, but slow down a bit."

She tried, for all the good it did. "I don't … Pip, what are you getting at?"

With a silent breath of frustration, Alice put a finger to her lip then pulled it down in the sign for *red*, followed by pinching her thumb and pointer together at her temple.

"Go on," I whispered, and my heart sped up. I suspected I knew the direction she was headed.

She made the sign for Y, a closed fist with her thumb and pinky stuck out, gave it two twists, then repeated the pinching sign by her forehead. The one that meant hair.

Red hair.

Yellow hair.

We could sneak in. Alice knew how because she'd done it before. With a little help.

"Oh, Pip," I said. "That's brilliant."

"Care to let me in on the secret?" asked Nola.

I told her, rapid-fire and a little overexcited. As the short version of the story wrapped up, I found myself slowing with a trace of worry rattling around my tone. I shook my head. "They can get us in, and I bet they would, but once inside, they can't hide us. We'd be on our own, sneaking around and hoping for the best. We'd need some kind of … I don't know. Distraction, I guess."

A heavy hopelessness fell over the room and for the better part of five minutes, we sat watching each other, waiting for someone's eyes to go wide with inspiration. Nothing but dull thoughtfulness until Alice nearly spilled out of her seat again.

Barely able to keep from hopping as she did it, she laid her left hand flat, palm up, and waved her right hand over the top. Once I nodded in understanding, she gave us the second word, a double snap using her middle finger.

"What?" asked Nola. "What is it?"

"I don't—" Boy, I felt particularly useless that day. "Song dog. She's signing 'song dog.' Pip, I don't get it. What—"

Nola let out a fierce exhale and dropped her cigarette. Color rose in her cheeks. "I think I might know what she's spinning around. And Mr. Daggett, that is one bright girl you have there."

CHAPTER 17

SARSAPARILLA

Thad demonstrated considerable reluctance to the idea. His face teased worry, and sent me away believing he just didn't want to feel left out. After all, his role in the whole affair was to oversee a swearing-in ceremony and try his damnedest to make it run long. A thorough job of that combined with a little luck and we might even be able to break up the evening with a dramatic entrance. Hell, maybe even kick down the door of the sheriff's office and drop some damning piece of evidence on the desk.

Eventually, with a hearty sigh, Thad relented and promised to buy us as much time as possible and to even go easy on sentencing me and Alice if we got caught snooping. The jail time didn't worry me too much. I'd seen the dead-eyed look on Big Lou's face, the way the Pinkerton fella outside longed to itch his finger on the trigger of his rifle, the kind of look that said maybe he wasn't actually employed with the agency anymore.

"I'm not sure you have to worry about them hauling us down to the jail if we get caught," I told Thad.

He simply nodded. The gleam in his eye reinforced my thinking that he wanted to tag along. Frankly, I wished he could. Who better than a consulting detective to peek around a man's place of business and detect? In the end, he settled for wishing me and Alice luck.

As we'd suspected, the vote count came out just about the same as the first go-round, certainly nowhere near enough change to avoid the next step in the process. Making a public announcement. As a rule, when Buzzard's Edge held an election, there was a bit of transition time. I'll be damned if I knew how much, since I never had reason to pay attention to it before. Under current circumstances, however, Thad planned to make the announcement that very afternoon and hold the swearing-in the next night.

In other words, get your plan together in one hell of a hurry, Daggett, and thank whatever lives up in the sky you don't have enough time to overthink it.

Of course, I didn't need the good luck Thad graced us with. I had Alice.

Along with a few things to do before the next night.

The schoolhouse door stood propped open, letting in a hint of breeze. Not a sound from inside. All the kids had run on home just a few minutes earlier. I glanced in the doorway to find Hazel Kane alone at her desk, head down, lost in a book.

"Now, the last time I was in here, there was a man on that there desk being carved up by some fellas with a grudge against him."

She scooted her chair back, startled, then looked up and fixed me with a warm smile. "I do hope that's not a memory from your own time here," she said. "You're Buzzard's Edge born and raised, right? You must've gone here."

"No to both, actually." I ran a hand through my hair and took a few steps toward her desk to buy some time, figure whether or not I was expected to go on. "My mother, my first mother, a lovely woman filled with the kind of love this world seems to mostly lack, she schooled me at home for the first part of my life."

If Hazel thought the term "first mother" odd, she kept it to herself. "Where'd you go after?"

"Well, nowhere really." I hesitated; saw the way she looked at me. The smile had slipped off her face. Not like she was upset, more like that near-blank, studious look a person sometimes gets when they're listening. Really listening. A bit of something like trust kindled in my chest right about then. "See, when I was a little younger than Alice, a man named George Holcomb rode up alongside a train I was on with my parents. He robbed the passengers blind, then executed everyone on board. All except me."

It was a familiar story in the town, one it seemed everybody knew, although before the whole hero thing they usually avoided my gaze anyhow. The way Hazel's face dropped, and her eyelids peeled back, it was clear she'd never heard it before.

"You hid?" she asked somewhere beneath a whisper.

A moment passed, and I considered saying yes. It was less nasty than the truth. Hell, I could even pretend I hadn't seen my daddy's brains go flying out the window. The "yes" was halfway to my lips when I decided I didn't want to lie to this woman. Not even to shield her from something rotten.

"It happened so fast there wasn't time to hide. I guess my ma and daddy would've hid me if they could have. I wonder about that sometimes. Holcomb—" I chewed my lip. "They called him 'Noose' and for his own reasons, he let me live."

When she spoke, it wasn't a gush of sorry's or you-poor-thing's. "What an awful thing to have to live with," was all she said.

"There's been times I said the same. Then I think of the other way it could've gone. A blood-soaked train rolling back into Buzzard's Edge, not a soul left alive on board, and nobody to chase down old Noose and hold him to account."

I didn't expand on the meaning there, but I saw in her eyes she got it. As I said, I wasn't about to lie. That didn't mean sharing every grisly detail.

"I didn't know."

"Yep," I said, letting my eyes wander out the open doorway. "Now you do. Maybe I'll tell you about Alice's story one day, how we ended up together. Maybe she might even be the one to share it."

Hazel nodded and I could see written on her face she'd at least known Alice wasn't actually my daughter. Not by blood, at least. Despite my doubt, it seemed the whispers were still alive and well in the town. Or maybe I'd gone off at the mouth the other night and just forgot about it.

I laughed out an ill-fated attempt to lighten the mood. "So, yeah, I never came to this schoolhouse. Don't even know anything about the guy they named it after. Josiah Dennis, isn't it? I knew a lot of the kids that went here but got most of my education at home. After that, working a farm with my adoptive parents, Willie and Henry Taff."

She didn't ask what had happened to them, which was alright, since I was almost talked out and I hadn't even sat down yet.

"Interesting. Is that why you're hesitant to let Alice join the class?"

The question caught me by surprise and I'm afraid I let my face show it. "Am I hesitant?"

Hazel shrugged. "That's just my read. You didn't have her in school even when your friend was running the classroom."

At that, I grabbed the closest chair, too small by half, and took a load off. "Believe it or not, Thad and me weren't all that close before the Devil's Cavern thing. I thought he was a prick, and he thought I was a rapscallion. If you can believe that."

Stifling a laugh, she brushed a strand of hair behind her ear. "Doubling down, Rory. It'd be good for her. But you didn't come all the way down here to tell your story or have me pick on you when life's juggling all these complications." Her smile dulled a little, but only a little. "Results from the vote in yet?"

I let my eyes fall to the student desk in front of me. Some kid had carved a few gouges that appeared almost like letters. Nothing I could read.

"Oh no," she whispered. "Really?"

Without looking up, I nodded. "Counted twice and everything. Thad's making the announcement pretty soon here. Making it all official tomorrow."

She groaned. "I'm sorry. I should never have encouraged you to run."

I met her eye and waved her words away. "Nah, you can stop all that. First off, you were hardly alone in bending my ear, and second ..." I paused, trying to put the words in the right order. "I couldn't sit back and do nothing. I'd never heard of the guy, then all of a sudden, I'm bowled over with stories and feelings about how bad the fucker is." I shrugged. "I couldn't do nothing."

A curious glint sparked in her eye. They were this lovely shade of brown, light as tanned leather, with flecks of green dotting them like stars. "That's past tense," she said, softly, like it was to herself. "But you're not giving up, are you?"

That picture of Mary McHugh spun around my head again, pretending to come on to me just to get close enough to shove in the knife. Made it real hard to trust a person.

With a sigh, I said, "I like you, Hazel. Quite a bit, in fact. Feels like you get me."

"Rory Daggett." There was caution in her tone, with just a touch of mischief. "What are you up to?"

I figured I knew her answer before I even asked the next question.

"Reason I came down here," I said, "was to put you out. See if you might be willing to help with something you got a talent for."

The concern in her tone spread across her face. That mischief, though? That stayed put in those brown and green eyes of hers.

"I'll get down on my knees and beg if I have to," I said.

Alice and me sat out on the porch that night, sipping at the jug of sarsaparilla Hazel had brought us ages ago. Sweet, spicy, with a hint of licorice and wintergreen. It hit just right. The wind died down around the same time the moon started peeking out, and after eating half our weight in bean burritos, we needed a little fresh air. Small, that girl might be, but her gut packed a punch, and she wasn't shy about it.

For a long time, we relished the silence, the light whoosh of a stray wind gust, the far-off howl of a coyote. A distant song came from either the town kicking up a ruckus or insects looking for mates. In this special brand of isolation, it could've been either and I kind of liked not knowing.

"You don't have to come, Pip. Not if you don't want to." I said it because my own conscience told me I had to. I knew she wouldn't take me up on it. Not in a hundred years' worth of chances. Truth was, the whole idea of aiming the kid like a gun had been on my mind lately, ever since we were holed up waiting for the election results and got to talking. I needed this to be her call.

Alice cracked a smile and held her fist to her forehead, pinky raised.

"Well, that was kind of rude."

That near-silent, gravelly laugh. Kid had a high opinion of her own sense of humor.

"I keep thinking it over and I can't come up with much we need to bring. I've got matches, handkerchiefs, that pocketwatch Nola lent us. None of those'll take up much room. 'Course we'll bring our revolvers, some extra bullets, and I figured we could each secret away a knife. Never know, they might come in handy. Hazel and Nola will bring the rest. Hey, might not be a bad idea to empty this thing and bring it with us."

I lifted the half-empty jug and took a gulp. "In a perfect world, we're in and out, nobody the wiser." I let out an impressive belch. "But the world's pretty far from perfect."

Alice made her pointer and middle fingers into a V and jutted them out, then put her right hand over her left wrist.

I shook my head. "I get it. I'd love to give Vivian and Drea a warning. I mean, if they're not working tomorrow or unwilling to help, we're on our own, but I don't think it's worth the risk being seen there. Nah, Pip, hard as it is, I think we gotta just sit and wait."

We let the silence creep back in, like I'd given an instruction rather than an unpleasant truth, watching the darkness pool around the edges of the desert. Frequently, I checked for monstrous eyes, listened for anything outside of the sounds of a normal desert night. Nothing untoward ever came. Evidently Alexander Farrell found himself too busy to set the dogs loose on the likes of us. Either that or the moment he won, he forgot we even existed.

Chapter 18

A Ticking Pocketwatch

The next night, me and Alice snuck down side streets, keeping to the shadows. A wholly unnecessary ploy, as it turned out, because there wasn't a soul to be seen anywhere in the damn town. There's always eyes in Buzzard's Edge, sure, sure, but with that in mind, I kept a lookout on every window, and each one sure seemed deserted to me.

We snuck past the sheriff's office and found its lights doused. Odd at first until we realized they must have moved the swearing-in ceremony. My heart missed a tick as I imagined the Scarlet Revolver, packed to bursting with half the town celebrating Farrell's victory. Yet, tonight was the night, so I swallowed hard and onward we went until we ran out of main street.

At the corner where the main street branched off into two smaller roads, we ducked down next to Beaumont's Leather shop, a crowded location during the day. On the night of a big old shindig, however? It's like I said, not a soul.

Most locals called the road that went left off main, Front Street. Down its stretch a couple buildings and on the right, the Scarlet Revolver was clearly open for business. Far from hopping, though.

Out front, the Pinkerton scowled under a warm drizzle of lantern light, clutching his rifle like he was trying to cut off its air supply. His gaunt face appeared so pissy, you might expect he thought the boss was watching, judging his general unfriendliness.

A guard outside meant business inside. Nola was right about at least one thing. Arrogance breeds predictability. I slipped her pocketwatch into the moonlight to check the time and, as if on cue, a soft *clink* like wood against an empty bottle sounded a little way down Front Street.

The guard turned his head.

Alice and me shot across the road like flame down a fuse, padding as quietly as possible while also hoping Mr. Pink didn't decide to go investigate. Once concealed beside the Scarlet Revolver, I risked a look out. There he stood under the glow of lantern light, just as bitchy looking, but without much hint of curiosity.

A moment passed as I searched the shadowy alleys between the buildings on the opposite side of the road, finally spotting Nola and Hazel directly across from the saloon, tucked into an alley on the other side of Beaumont's. The *clink* had come from a bit farther down the road, so I guessed they had no trouble navigating the narrow alleyways between buildings, and that was alright.

The ladies crouched behind a half-rotten section of fence that made them perfectly clear to me and Alice but hidden from Mr. Pink's line of sight. Once seen, Hazel sported a big grin, clearly having developed a taste for the clandestine. She closed her right fist with the thumb sticking out and placed her left hand in the same position on top.

Against my side, I felt Alice rumble with silent laughter. Hazel had her hands switched, and it wasn't quite the way you were supposed to use "all set" but bless her, she tried. I shot back a simple "yes." A closed fist in a nodding motion.

"Now or never, Pip," I whispered. "You could still sneak back and stay with them."

She brushed her thumb along the right side of her jaw twice.

"Think Viv and Drea wouldn't let me in by myself? You underestimate my charm."

I held out the backs of my hands and wiggled my fingers at Hazel. "Wait," it said, then we slipped down the dark passage alongside the saloon. I put a hand on Alice's shoulder to guide her in front. My free hand rested on the butt of my revolver.

"Lead the way," I said, between gritted teeth. We favored stealth over haste, pressed against the building, one soft step at a time until we came to the corner. A drift of voices cut around the bend and forced us flat to the wall like a gaggle of horned lizards. A moment, two, and I counted each voice as belonging to a woman. Hushing my tongue, I gave Alice a look that I hoped said, *Is that them?*

She pushed off the wall and walked around the corner with the kind of confidence you only see from folks on a stage.

"Allie!" came a muffled cry, and a weight I hadn't realized I was carrying dropped from my shoulders. I followed Allie, as she was affectionately known around this place, and by some kind of divine providence, found her in the company of Vivian and Drea. None of the other girls who might raise an eyebrow or an alarm. The two ladies sat on overturned crates, their shoes on the ground next to them as they rubbed each other's feet. And here I thought they weren't spending much time on them.

I smiled at them, keeping that last idea to myself, and saw them darken in fear before it turned to relief and recognition.

"Allie's daddy," said Vivian. "You looked different under the moonlight, not all bathed in smoke. 'Course there's no mistaking this kid here." She pinched at Alice's cheeks playfully as Drea burst into laughter. My heart ached a little seeing her giggle. I wouldn't dare to pin a number on either girl except to say they were both younger than I first thought. Turned out they looked a bit different under the moonlight, as well.

"What are you two doin' out here at night?" asked Drea, some flat suspicion in her voice.

Alice turned to me, handing me the lead after that strut onstage. I chewed on my lip, second guessing the line we'd worked out. "We were hoping to get inside, and that maybe you two lovely ladies might help us with that."

The way they looked at each other spoke of closeness. An entire conversation passed through the way one girl made eye contact and the other tilted her head.

"Why?" asked Vivian.

Taking my hat off and holding it in front of my chest, I said, "Might be better if you all didn't know."

Another one of those looks, a thousand silent words.

"And you want us to just trust you?" asked Drea. "We don't even know you."

"Fair play," I said, and readied myself for the risk. "But you know who I am. I'd bet on that. And you should probably know I'm not too friendly with the fella who runs this establishment. I didn't miss the looks on your faces when you thought we might mention your names to him." I chewed at the inside of my cheek, then went for the center of the dartboard. "And I ain't forgot the names of your friends, either. Mina and Celeste, wasn't it?"

There it was. The words seemed to hang in the air as the girls passed one more look, a little extra eyebrow, some smacked lips, and puckered cheeks this time. Still no words. When they turned back, it wasn't to me.

"Allie?" asked Vivian.

Alice lifted her hands to say something, then held them fast. Instead, she knelt down and scratched in the dirt.

I leaned in with interest. I might've gone for a guarantee that we wouldn't rat them out or that we wouldn't get caught and cost them their jobs. Or worse. Instead, she went with nobility. Appeal to their better nature over self-preservation.

Interesting, indeed.

"We could help a lot of people," it read.

When Alice had finished writing, she stood and brushed her hands against her pants, small streams of sand falling to the ground, then waited for a response.

Drea folded her arms in front of her chest and sucked her teeth.

Vivian struck a similar pose. This time they both looked at me, a glare so heavy I could feel it on my shoulders. "Doubt there's much you could do for Mina and Celeste, save maybe givin' their mommas a straight answer to what happened to 'em."

"What if we could stop it from happening again?" My stomach went cold with the weight of that promise; one I wasn't anywhere near sure I could keep.

Vivian didn't answer, but allowed a trace of hope to touch her eyes.

"It's pretty empty tonight," said Drea. "Lots of people down at the general store hootin' it up. Might be a smaller chance of gettin' you all caught."

Gratitude hopped to the back in favor of curiosity. "McGregor's General?" I asked. "Why there?"

"Where else?" asked Vivian, a sly smile taking over her face. "Sheriff's office is too small, and the only other saloon in town burned to the ground. I mean, Mr. Locke suggested we have it here. Drea heard him."

"I heard it," she confirmed.

Interesting, I thought. Maybe Thad had designs on helping from the inside. Sure would've been an ugly surprise for us.

"Only Alex, he said no, no, no and waved it off. Said it would not be appropriate for him to profit off the townspeople celebrating their new mayor."

"He's not wrong," I said, with caution.

Vivian leaned forward and fluttered her eyebrows. "He could've set out drinks for free. "

"Or lowered the cost to just break even if his pockets were feeling tight," added Drea.

"And Locke didn't push it." Vivian again. She giggled and went on. "But if you're here when almost no one else is, I would bet ..." she jabbed in the chest with her pointer finger. "That you think the same thing as us."

Drea rested her chin on her clasped hands. "That he's got something worth hiding."

I thought it safer not to say anything. Alice agreed.

Hopping to her feet, Vivian twirled in a clumsy spin that told of either a lack of grace or a few shots of moonshine. "Once we're in, you're on your own. We don't know you; you don't know us. If Lou or that scary fucker out front catch you, Drea and me will run on back to our rooms and let 'em shoot you dead."

"Charming of you, but understandable," I said.

"You can stay with me if they shoot your daddy, Allie." Drea flapped her skirt and started toward the back entrance. "I don't think they'd shoot a kid. At least Lou wouldn't. The other guy?" She shrugged. "Hope you're good at hiding."

"Well, then, uh, thank you both. One thing I gotta do, then we'd sure appreciate your help." Without waiting for an answer, I slinked back around the building to the mouth of the alleyway. Nola and Hazel were no longer behind the fence. I knew they'd be watching, though. As silently as I could, I pulled a matchbook from my pocket, struck one, and stuck it head-up in the dirt. A little torch against the darkness and a ticking pocketwatch.

Chapter 19

Camptown Races

Compared to the simplicity of the Saloon of the End of the World, the off-limits-to-the-public area of the Scarlet Revolver was a downright labyrinth, somehow seeming bigger on the inside. Hastily constructed hallways with nails sticking out along the edges made for the kind of entrance only the help would use. A series of shoddily mounted lanterns kept us from complete darkness, barely shimmering enough light forth to help navigate the endless twists and turns.

Vivian and Drea held hands, walking just ahead with the surefire speed of a duo who could round these bends in their sleep.

"The way the wood bounces sound," whispered Vivian. "If anyone's coming the other way, we'll get plenty of warning."

I nodded, grateful. It was like she'd read my mind.

We'd bumbled through about a hundred miles of hallway and were likely only fifteen feet into the building, at least as the crow flies, when the first sound came. A *shump* like a stomped boot made Viv and Drea stop in their tracks, still like marble statues. Even with the dull, flickering firelight, I could see the color drain from their faces. They froze only for a moment before regaining some composure. A quick squeeze of their hands, then Viv set forward while Drea took a step back.

"Ready to run back the way we came. Just not yet," she whispered.

Vivian disappeared around the corner. "Oswald!" she said in the most mock pleasant voice I'd ever heard.

Drea tensed, her eyes going dark. Whoever this Oswald character was, he clearly left a sour impression on both girls. She braced her hands against the wall like she could cover me and Alice up with her slender arms. If there was a signal to turn and dash for open air, I missed it.

The response to Vivian's spirited greeting was thick and mumbled, barely intelligible. "Sweet ass doin' in a dark hole like this 'un" was the closest I could get.

"No need to be a charmer, Ozzie. Just comin' in from a little fresh air. Real question is, what are you doin' down this way?" Her voice dropped but kept its sweetness. "Lou'll stove your head in he catches you wandering 'round the back again."

"Last time he wouldn't serve me for a week!" the man cried.

"Well, then, y'all better turn tail and scoot back, shouldn't ya? I can't accept no coin from a man who ain't allowed inside. Know what I mean?"

"Ahhhh, fuck." Then a clattering bang that made all three of us jump.

"Oswald Harris, you clumsy oaf," she said in a chiding tone. It sounded practiced and maybe because some fellas liked to be talked to that way. "You head on back for one more round. Nurse it nice and slow, then tell Lou I said to point you to my room. Ain't nobody in there tonight. Second thought, make it two rounds. You got enough for a couple more drinks with a little left over for me?"

"Reckon I do." The gruff, surly voice came from low down, like he was still laid out on the floor. He groaned as he climbed to his feet, then his big old boot clomps headed in the opposite direction.

When Vivian reappeared, she was fiddling with her hands and trembling. "I've seen that look on him before. It ain't a nice one. Any luck and two more drinks'll put him over the top. He can sleep it off in my room. I ball up his slacks on the floor and he'll expect he got what he paid for." The whole time she talked, her eyes wandered, finding nobody. "With some luck."

Drea pulled her in and squeezed her tight. "I doubt there'll be anyone waiting on me. I can hang around and help you."

Vivian nodded, then her gaze found me and Alice. Her eyes went rabbit-wide like she'd forgotten us. "I think we'd better part here. That was a little too close for comfort. Give us a minute or two to get ahead, then just keep following this hallway. It'll kick you out into the saloon proper. You keep to the shadows, you should be able to sneak past Lou, get upstairs. That's where you're going, ain't it?"

She asked it in a tone that didn't seem to require an answer.

"If we see anybody coming down this way, we'll give you a whistle," said Drea. "*Camptown Races* or something fun like that."

I tipped my hat. "Appreciate you bringing us this far, and don't you worry. Nobody'll know we were here."

After a quick search for some dust to write in, Alice settled for signing a "thank you." Before I could translate, she rushed forward and wrapped each of the girls in a hug. Something passed between the three of them, though I couldn't judge quite what it was. By then, I figured Alice didn't need me to pass on her gratitude.

"Hey," I said awkwardly. "You're good souls for this. Ever need anything, you can find us just outside of town. A couple miles past the southwest line. Don't be shy, you hear?"

Without a word, they both turned and set off to deal with Ozzie, who likely was sat at the bar by now, guzzling rather than nursing that drink.

With the girls out of sight, I turned to Alice and whispered, "We'll give 'em a minute. Can't swing much more. I'd love to trust to the shadows, but I'll take planning over luck any day."

From my back pocket, I took a pair of handkerchiefs, one black and one dyed such a dark shade of blue, it might as well have been black. Alice took one, and we both tied them around our faces. At least if we got caught in a passing glance, whoever saw us wouldn't know who we were. Thinking back on it, there probably weren't all that many sneak thieves who palled around with kids. Even with Alice's hair pinned up and tucked into her hat, they might know who to come looking for.

Too late. We'd have to deal with that fire when it caught the dry chaff.

As we set out, I listened for the telltale whistle of "Camptown Races," "Oh Susanna!," or any other Stephen Foster song that might occur to Drea in a moment of panic. No warning, so the way must be clear.

A couple more twisty turns and the hallway cleared up a little, even deigning to run in a straight line for more than a few feet. No loose nails sticking out of the wall and the lanterns no longer seemed in danger of sputtering out. The sounds of clinking glasses and murmured conversations drifted our way, telling us the scenery changed because we were close to the customers.

No more talking at this point. Maybe trouble for some. Our partnership, however, had its own language, which produced less sound than the rustle of clothes and some displaced air. I braced Alice back with an outstretched palm and stepped lightly, testing each floorboard before committing my weight. I hadn't noticed any squeakers in the maze we'd passed through. Didn't mean there wasn't one farther on, ready to rat us out.

I couldn't remember seeing a back hallway the first time we'd come here, but then again, I wasn't looking for it. Putting as little of myself as possible on display, I peeked out to survey the room. The back hallway emptied into the saloon directly across from the bar, where Big Lou stood behind the counter, polishing another glass that didn't seem primed to accept it. Another step out of the shadows and he couldn't miss me. Leaned against the bar, sat a man that looked more like the Mogollon monster than I cared for. I took him to be Ozzie Harris. The neat row of empty glasses before him, not to mention the way he wobbled on his stool, told me he wouldn't be a threat. Scattered around the room were several others. A few somber patrons occupied stools on either side of Harris. Far to my left, an older fella with a droopy mustache was positioned in front of the piano, staring off into nothing. Evidently, he'd decided the crowd didn't call for music.

The staircase that led to Farrell's office was to my right, a fifteen-foot expanse of wall away. Unfortunately, there seemed just about no way of getting there without Lou or one of those gents, as deep in their cups as they might be, noticing.

I drew back and held up six fingers to Alice, one for each potential firearm that might be aimed at us if we fucked up, then fished out Nola's pocketwatch. "Any time now," I muttered under my breath, then cursed myself for breaking the silence. I sat still as a scared sand cat, waiting for my heart to drop back down to a normal tempo. Alice did the same. We could've passed for a painting if someone happened by at that moment.

When I granted enough time had passed, I poked my head out again and caught Lou looking in my direction, eyebrows wrinkled over his squinty eyes. Ducking back, I plastered myself against the wall and drew my revolver.

Barely in the door, Daggett, and already in a position to shoot your way out.

I listened for a lull in conversation, a pulled-back pistol hammer, pounding bootsteps.

Instead, I heard sweet music. Not from the piano. No. Clattering through the walls came a series of pops, almost like gunfire, one after another. The tinkle of broken glass accompanied each glorious bang. Even hearing them through the walls, they were louder than I expected, each boom sounding from a different direction, like we were surrounded.

"Oops." I shot Alice a grin, then held my hand up again, waiting.

A muffled "Shit!" came from far away. Maybe Mr. Pink, maybe Agatha. Either way, it had the intended effect. Stools and a piano bench skidded across the wood floor and an army of running footsteps barreled out the front entrance.

Nola and Hazel had done their job beautifully.

Chapter 20

Lightning Bug Piss

The idea belonged to Nola, lord only knows where she got it. I wasn't about to ask. The jugs came from Hazel, turned out the free time she devoted to pottery was all kinds of productive. According to Nola, you fill some old jugs with kerosene and seal 'em tight with a strip of cloth. After that, you light the end of the material on fire, and depending on how much fuse you leave, give yourself enough time to get clear.

Now, if you plan all that just right, and put one of those jugs in the mouth of every alley surrounding a certain saloon, a team of just two women sounds a whole lot like a full-blown army.

Not unlike a couple of song dogs making themselves sound like a big old pack to stay alive.

Sure seemed the pack Alice and me started up had a couple more members these days.

Once the saloon sounded clear, some of the ladies who worked up on the second floor poured down the stairs to make sure they weren't under siege. An unexpected development, but a welcome one for sure. Not a single one of them went for the back hallway, so the top floor would presumably be either empty or occupied by women who shut themselves in their rooms waiting for the danger to pass.

We had a clear path to Farrell's office and took it. Up the stairs and down the hallway, no tiptoeing or checking for whiny floorboards. Each room we skirted by stood stark empty or with its door closed, likely locked.

Fuck.

Feet away from Farrell's office at the end of the hallway, I stopped in my tracks, bunching up the fancy carpet and drawing a concerned look from Alice.

"What do you want to bet that door is locked, Pip? Pretty fair chance, I'd say."

She went a little gray and mimed a kick.

"Unless you think you could repair it while I look around, that'd be a pretty loud calling card to show Farrell he's had visitors."

Shaking my head, I eyed up the handle on the office door. "Looks like a warded lock," I said with a chuckle. "My daddy had one of these on his work shed. If we had—" I snapped my fingers. "Pip, you got anything holding your hair up besides that hat?"

A flicker of confusion, then a spark of imagination. Alice pushed her hat back off her head and reached up to pull out a two-headed brass contraption with a star attached to the end. As soon as she held it out, her blonde hair fell down past her shoulders.

"Ah, you're brilliant, kid." I snatched the hairpin and hoped to hell it was slender enough to do the job. "It's been some time, but if I remember right, it's all about patience and motion." Tongue stuck out to the side, I dropped to one knee and started in. Alice turned to face the stairway, revolver holstered but her hand ready to pull at a moment's notice.

From the end of the hallway, the lone staircase, a series of voices floated up. Too far to make out any words clearly. The tone sounded blustery and upset. Alice's hairpin squeezed in no problem, and I started to twist. Slowly, slowly, feeling for anything that could pass for a catch.

A tap came at my shoulder. When I turned, Alice made two finger guns and fake fired them. It took a moment for my mind to catch up and see it as the sign for "fast" rather than Alice asking permission to gun down anyone who had the nerve to climb the stairs.

"Yeah, thanks, Pip. I'm hurrying and it ain't a science." Though I wasn't sure that was true.

Rotate little by little and nothing. A warded lock, sure, but not every one was designed the same. A clunk sounded and my heart leapt, thinking I had it, until I realized the sound had come from the first footstep on the stairs. Farrell's girls returning after running outside and finding nothing more exciting than pottery shards.

Wide-eyed, Alice dropped her pretend guns in favor of a real one. Still turning the hairpin, I whispered, "Pip, don't shoot. Might even be Viv and Drea. That ain't no way to say thanks."

She lowered the gun, but didn't holster it. In my head, I vowed to stop turning around so damn much. Not even when another stair creaked, one that sounded about halfway up. We could trust Viv and Drea to clam up, I'd wager that, but asking them to swear all Farrell's other girls to secrecy seemed too big of an ask.

Sweat dripped down my temple. "Come on, you fucker," I whispered through gritted teeth. Another footstep. Then I felt it catch. No mistaking it this time. Careful not to rotate any farther, I added a light bit of pressure. The click resonated more than sounded, but it was enough. I gave the handle a turn, relief flooding into my body like a cool breath. I ducked inside with Alice right behind me and eased the door shut. No sooner did door meet frame than those footsteps hit the carpet that ran the length of the hallway. I held my breath, thinking anyone looking in the right direction might've seen the door close. Those footsteps found their way to individual rooms, lowered voices whispering conspiracies before guttering out, replaced by closed doors.

Alice and me both let out a big breath at the same time and reengaged the lock before setting out. "Assume we're not rolling in time," I said.

In response, she holstered her gun and slapped two flat arms against one another.

"Me?" I asked, and she shot back a quick nod, then set to combing over the various shelves pressed up against the walls, leaving me to sort through the controlled chaos of Farrell's desk.

Stacks upon stacks of papers decorated the big oak desk. Yellowed, old, and mostly lists of figures. Dull and nearly unintelligible, the kind of things you could leave in plain sight because most folks, including myself, would write it off as business as usual. Nowhere near enough time to read every line and look for inconsistencies, but maybe Thad would still push for that financial transparency I tried to sell the town. A quick shuffle through the pile. It all looked the same.

Fuck it.

I turned my attention to the desk drawers, patting my pocket for Alice's hairpin, at the same time hoping I wouldn't need to use it again. Another breeze of relief settled in when I saw the drawers had no locks.

What am I even looking for? I thought as I reached for the top drawer. *More coins? Maybe one with a little, red-eyed wolf monster, a goddamn skunk ape?*

With each drawer I sifted through, relief gave way to frustration. More papers in drawer number one, a couple tumbler glasses and a bottle of rotgut in drawer number two. Drawer number three. Something good must be in there. I threw it open, and my stomach sank low enough to hit the ground floor.

More fucking papers. These ones I recognized as purchase orders. I thumbed through them to discover a pistol and some spare rounds underneath. My pulse didn't even jump at that. All it meant was he hadn't taken his firearm to the party. Grasping at straws, I picked up the stack of purchase orders. Front and center on the top of the pile, it read "Cactus Cat" with a price tag of $250.

"What the fu—"

My voice caught in my throat as I looked to Alice. I expected to find her digging through books or pocketing knickknacks to go with her chimera coin. At first, I didn't see her at all. Then I looked down.

That gray pallor she'd taken on in the hallway appeared worse, like a stone with a damp mop of blonde hair. She'd pulled down her handkerchief and was hunched up in something like the fetal position, ragged breaths hitching her chest. I dropped the papers back in Farrell's drawer and kicked the desk shut, then ran to her and cradled her head.

Poison, I thought. *He knew we were coming. Something sabotaged.*

Then Alice's eyes looked straight through me. I had one hand behind her head, the other under her lower back, and she couldn't see me a foot in front of her face. I knew this look, had seen it twice before, and it meant two things.

One, we had to go.

Two, someone was going to die tonight.

Once I'd scooped her up, I took a second to Locke-check the office, trying to channel his observant nature and make sure we hadn't left anything too fucked up. It looked fine, probably imperfect, but I needed to get her out of there. There'd be a crowd, so I pulled our handkerchiefs up to cover our faces before I opened the door. One-handed, I locked the mechanism and pulled it shut, hoping it would stay so, and at the same time, not really giving much of a fuck.

My little girl was hurting, and the second floor of a brothel wasn't the ideal setting for this kind of fit.

The doors all remained closed, so that was alright. We found a nice mix of hurry and soft padding that didn't draw attention, nor let us dally. One step at a time down the stairs, and when we hit the bottom, I hid us in the shadows and peeped out into the saloon proper. All the men were back like they'd never left their posts. Equally solemn and unsober. Thankfully, their attention was on their cups and not the path to the second floor.

I closed my eyes like it would help me think, listening to Alice breathing. It was closer to steady, no rasp. When I opened my eyes, her color was still sickly, her eyes distant.

What do we do, Pip?

I didn't dare speak it out loud.

If I walked into the saloon, turned my back the second I hit the light, I could hide Alice, and …

And what?

We couldn't go out the back. Drea and Viv said that was off limits to customers. I couldn't sneak Alice past them. What I needed was another distraction. How could I communicate that desire to Hazel and Nola? Did they even have any jugs left? Would it work twice?

I stifled a sigh and peered out again. All the same exits, all the same issues, except—

"Yeah, shut the fuck up, Harris, I'll check."

Lou put his dirty glass down with an angry *clank* and started in our direction, head turned toward the men at the bar for the moment.

Up or down, Daggett. Up or down.

With that stink climbing up from the basement, I took a chance on Lou wanting nothing to do with it and slid sideways, ducking under the rope and backing down the cellar stairs. They proved a little more rickety than the last set, but they were good secret keepers. Another step back. I was more worried about gagging at the smell that wafted up from below.

Lou stopped at the base of the stairs, one hand on the rope. All he had to do was look down, and we were fucked. I held my breath. He stood there for hours, days, then tilted his head up. "Viv! You up there? Ozzie says he's waiting for you."

Vivian's twang drifted from the top floor. "Give him another round. Put it on my tab." A pause. "Then I guess you can send him up, if he can still do stairs at that point."

Lou chuckled, a low growling sound that never escaped his chest. He stood there for another moment, then shook his head and fucked off back to the bar.

Despite the smell, I needed to lay Alice down for a moment, to think, and we were already half down the stairs. At the very least, I could have a look around. Hell, there might even be something down there to blow up and clear out the saloon, at least for a couple minutes.

The aroma relented when I stepped onto the bare-dirt cellar floor. Or maybe I just got used to it. Still hazy-eyed, Alice was in no shape to give her opinion. Shifting her to one arm, I dug out the book of matches and lit one, careful to block the light with my back to the stairs. It was surprisingly small down there, not much larger than Farrell's office. The walls were wooden, rather than dirt, and a few shelves lined three of them.

The shelves looked made of rotted logs with cobwebs holding them together, mostly cleaned off except for some jarred food that likely went bad back when Lincoln was taking in a play.

A pile of burlap sacks rested against one of the sturdier looking shelves and made for a comfy, yet scratchy, bed as I laid Alice down and rested a hand against her cheek. A little on the cool side, but still warm enough to keep me from worry. For now.

From above came the sound of piano, some brisk, choppy Mozart to move the hearts and minds of the men from the shower of ceramics outside. Likely it meant they were up and moving around. A couple footsteps and some unsettled dust raining from the ceiling told the truth of that.

"Shit, Pip."

Her breathing steadied enough to count as a response, and her hands jerked. Thumbs and pinkies out, then her arms crossed before falling to her side.

"Tonight," I whispered.

I pulled a sack over her like a blanket and snuffed out the first match, then lit a second and set to exploring. It wasn't a storeroom, not in the traditional sense. Anything down there earned its place at the hands of an employee too damn lazy to drag it out back to a burn pile. The irony was that the room lacked anything to burn.

So, that was plan A crumpled up and pitched into the privy.

After a thorough and frustrating search, the match guttered out, and after a peek at Alice, I let it. Conservation and all that. It left us alone in the dark with no escape plan and a pungent reek that made me wonder if maybe this was where Farrell had buried the bodies.

I shuddered the thought away.

Funny how things shake out, because I believe if I tried to hold onto the light, I might've missed our chance at freedom. In the pitch darkness, though, the place I vaguely remembered being the southwest corner of the room flickered like a jet of lightning bug piss dripping down the wall. A seam or a crack, with light on the other side. As I stepped closer, I felt a breeze. Warm and bathed in that rotting stink, barely more than a breath. Still, it left me without enough doubt to pull myself up by.

Another step forward, I reached out toward the light, then caught myself.

Alice, defenseless and not altogether with it.

I felt my way to her in the dark and took her hand. "I don't know how well you can hear me, Pip, but I think I might have found us a way out.

Now, I don't expect anyone to come down here, but I'm going to cover you up, and leave you that six-shooter of yours. Anybody bothers you, you be sure to teach 'em what a skull looks like when you turn it inside out." I felt for her other hand and moved it to her holster. "Thatta girl. I won't be gone long. Just want to scope it out and make sure it's safe. Then I'll come back for you. Promise." Her chest rose and fell, steady as you like, her eyes watching something overhead. Then two words echoed through my head.

Walk down.

Well, fuck, down the steps and into the cellar. I'd just have to be extra careful.

I went to stand, then on a whim I tapped my right hand against my chest, clapped it softly against my left, and spread both hands apart like opening a curtain. Dark or not, she likely couldn't see it, but I felt better for saying it.

You're all I have.

Then I thought about Hazel and Nola somewhere outside and wondered how true that was. For both of us.

CHAPTER 21

OUT TO PASTURE

Opening up that seam in the wall was easy. It was performing the task quietly that made for the challenge. However, some patience and a little help from the piano player switching from Mozart to Beethoven lined up all the gears.

I hadn't noticed the hinges built into the wall, even with a pretty thorough inspection of the room, so three cheers to the stinky cellar's architect. Once the door opened on a lantern-lit tunnel, the smell hit full bore. Less the smell of death and more shit and animal musk. Truth be told, it reminded me of Mogey. I secured the handkerchief over my mouth and nose, pulled my revolver, and set forward with a single thought on my mind.

The other side of the wall opened into something like a mine. Dirt walls climbed a couple feet over my head to a rounded, cavernous ceiling. Wooden support beams stood every so often to keep the whole mess from caving in on itself, with a lantern dangling off an iron nail pounded into the first one.

No way they keep this lantern lit all the time, I thought. *Somebody's down here.*

All the more reason to take the lantern with me. I hoisted it down from its perch and held it in front of me.

As I went on, hopes that any of the light shining through the crack into the cellar came from the moon started to dim. Unlit lanterns dangled every ten feet or so, but the only light came from the one in my hands. I couldn't help remembering the underground tunnel some fool had used to try and rob the bank. Only that was on the opposite end of town, and Billy Chambers had sealed it all up. This was something different. Larger, more permanent. You couldn't help admiring the handiwork that must've gone into hollowing this place out. Hadn't Nola said Farrell used to be in the mining business?

A low rumble sounded from up ahead, and I practiced some silent gratitude that I hadn't dragged Alice with me. The lantern light kept me from blindness, sure enough, but it hardly swept through the place like daylight.

My fingers tightened on the revolver's grip. A chill went up my spine, climbing like spiders at the echo. Had any other way out of that basement occurred to me at that moment, I would've turned and hauled tail back to Alice.

When that rumble drifted down the path again, I became sure. The earth wasn't caving in. Of course, that wasn't a positive across the board. Something was growling.

Cautious as a man scaling a cliff, I kept forward, revolver held high and shaking in the lantern light. A pair of red eyes opened in the dark up ahead, at first seeming to glow, before I realized they were catching the little bit of flame that cut through the dark.

Animal eyes.

After "walk down" it was the second sign, and there I was, alone. One person. All that remained was for one of the beasts behind those eyes to leave me choking on my own blood.

"Fuck me." I swallowed hard and turned to run. Something stopped me, though. Another growl. Mad as hell. Thing was, the rumble didn't come any closer. To the side of the first pair of eyes, a second set opened, content to watch from that distance.

Don't push your luck, Daggett.

Was their anger in those eyes or curiosity? A cautious warning?

As I approached, the eyes vanished behind a set of rusty iron bars. Someone had chipped a great mouth into the dirt and stone, then barred it up like a jail cell before dumping a group of critters in there. The dog-like snout and dark fur, spine ridging along the body, struck a bell. These were the same goat-sucking creatures that had killed Mrs. Rowles. Less fearsome locked up in the dark, for sure. This cage held three of them with enough room left over to house a fair few more. A couple days earlier, maybe it had.

"Son of a bitch," I whispered.

This is the point where I should turn around, check on Alice, find another way out the ground floor of the saloon.

Oh, Alice was going to be pissed at me.

Onward, and every ten feet or so, my lantern caught a bit of metal decorated with a little shine but mostly rust flecks. More bars, more cells.

Trapped behind the next set, and holding onto a sweet, earthy smell, was a monster that damn near stopped my heart. A lizard, it had to be, though I swear I'd never seen one a tenth that big before. It had the same black and orange coloring as a Gila monster, only this thing stretched out the size of my parlor, watching me with intelligence in one eye and a series of white scars on the other. I made sure to move slow, thinking that thing could probably take down those bars with a sweep of its tail if the mood struck.

"Good lord," I whispered. "You're the big fucker Nola talked about."

The big-as-a-bastard Gila monster blinked at me, slowly and in a way that said, "Move on, soldier" and I did.

Cages ranged from small to large, some with single animals, others with packs, every goddamn one of them something from a dream or a nightmare. There was a bobcat covered in quills like a porcupine.

Cactus Cat. I couldn't shake the thought.

Farther along, a different-looking cage. An iron door with a single barred window housed a couple of nasty-looking bright red worms, yellow spit dribbling from what I took to be their mouths, bodies that would run from shoulder to toe next to me. A long metal tool, like a branding iron, leaned against the bars. Something to poke at the worms and keep them in line, maybe. Alongside the door, it was plenty of warning not to venture too close.

One of the more normal looking creatures, except for its size, I recognized almost immediately. Another one that lived in Henry's stories. A dark-colored eagle stared out with keen eyes, black as death but with a lively shine to them. From talons to beak, it must've been as tall as me, and I could imagine its wingspan, only its cage wasn't wide enough for it to unfold its feathers.

"You're a Thunderbird, aren't you?"

No answer, not so much as a blink. Then again, I didn't really expect one.

Next door to the Thunderbird was a room with no door. A slab of table took up most of its length, doused in a dry brown substance I knew right away, least of all because of the dull buzz of flies who'd found their way down below ground. A series of knives and cleavers, enough different sizes to gut a whole host of animals, lay scattered across the blood-soaked table, and went a long way toward explaining the death part of the smell down there.

Only question was, what kind of beast got chopped up in that room? The kind of surface dwellers you needed to feed a collection of animals like this, or maybe a soiled dove put out to pasture.

Mina. Celeste.

A clump sounded from further down, and I froze, pressed against the wall. All for the best, maybe, because it pulled me back from the edge of wonder and set me to paying attention again, trying to figure a way out. Shifting movements and the occasional grunt of something living filled the underground tunnel. Just that.

Just a little farther before I give this up for a dead end.

The next cell, the most human-sized yet, held something that made my stomach hurt. If the Thunderbird was the most familiar of the bunch, this fella served as the most unsettling, mainly because it was the closest to human looking. Tall, two-legged, shiny like it was made of silver, and with a spade-shaped head. It didn't move, didn't even seem to breathe, so I passed on before it took notice.

Then came the first empty cell, making my heart race for a couple reasons. The open door and the lingering smell. Rot mixed with dead fish, somehow making it all the way back to the cellar of the Scarlet Revolver. At an easy ten feet tall, the doorway was big enough for Mogey, who either must be running around this underground sideshow or disappeared into the desert after I poked him in his big old eye.

If I kept walking, would I find freedom or that fire-breathing chimera from the burnt remains of the Saloon at the End of the World?

Farrell had one hell of a menagerie. His office might've turned up less than shit, but I wondered how the people of Buzzard's Edge'd feel about their mayor being behind a string of animal attacks.

As I stood at the entrance to Mogey's cage trying to decide whether to push on or head back to Alice, I never heard the footsteps behind me, never did know what hit me, sending the lantern scattering and stealing the light away.

CHAPTER 22

CHOKE

When I came to, it took a minute to figure where I was. Dim as dusk with a stink like a dead dog washed up in a river. How I ever lost consciousness with that smell assaulting my nostrils, I'll never know. Even accounting for the minimal light, the world seemed extra blurry. Beyond the bars of the closed door, stood a large figure. A single lantern, probably *my* lantern, hung from a support beam, its light not quite reaching him.

"Mr. Farrell," I said, stepping forward to give the door a shake. Locked. "Alex, if you like. I seem to have gotten myself trapped in here. Be a pal and let me out."

No answer, no movement.

"Is it because I didn't come to your celebration? Fine, I concede, and offer my most warm and heartfelt congratulations. Now open the fucking door." A jolt of fear and hope filled me. I reached down to my holster, nearly shouting in glee. Time or carelessness had caused him to leave me my revolver, so I pulled it and pointed it his way.

Then a few things happened at once.

The big man stepped forward, lantern light trickling over his face, revealing one nightmare bit at a time. My hand, already set to a tremble, had a full-on fit, and I lost hold of my revolver. A couple near-lucky juggles, then it smacked the cell bar and tumbled out, scattering to a rest on the dirt floor, just past what I expected I could reach. That's when I looked up.

For a second, I didn't know the man, but it sure as shit wasn't Alexander Farrell.

Tattered flesh ribboned along his swollen right cheek, like someone had stuffed a stick of dynamite in his mouth, lit the fuse, and ran. Jagged shards of teeth poked out, exposed to the air with only scraps of what used to be his lips covering them. Even under the dull light, I could tell the skin on that side of his face wasn't a healthy color, ranging from sick-bed gray to dark black like the mustache that only half-sat above his lip now. One bloodshot, jaundiced eye sunk into the ruined side of his face, peeking out over fleshy remnants like one of those hellish caged creatures glaring out from a cave. The smell coming off him made my stomach want to heave. A noxious mix of dead rodent and chicken eggs, both left out in the sun for days on end.

Diagnosis? Oh, I'd say if someone shot you in the face and you spent the next week underground with a bunch of animals, that'd about do it.

"Does Farrell know you're down here?" I asked, too impolite to stop staring.

Moses Harvey chuckled, at least I guess that's what it was supposed to be. To my ears, it was more like the sound a man might make choking to death on a gallon of sand.

"He doesn't even know I know about this place. Thinks it's some big secret. Like you can't smell the beasties from up in the saloon." His breathing was labored, and the good side of his face glowed a deep red. Exertion or infection. I had a guess.

"How can it be helped?" he asked. "When everyone who works for you learns to tell you what you want to hear all the time, you tend to forget what truth is."

I squeezed the bars and let my gaze slip down toward my revolver, wondering if I stuck my arm out as far as it would go, if I could reach it with my fingertips. Or if Harvey would kick it away before I had the chance.

"You killed my horse," I said.

"You killed my brother. S'pose that makes us square."

I shook my head. "I didn't kill him. If anything, we showed up to stop the trouble that night, whatever it was. Still kind of murky about it, if I'm honest. Besides, if you believed we were square, I suspect I wouldn't be locked in Mogey's cage."

He raised his one good eyebrow at the name, then understanding seemed to dawn.

"Answer me this at least," I said. "Was Farrell involved or is he just a shitheel all on his own accord?"

Harvey smiled, and it was so godawful looking I had to stare at the ground again. Quiet as it was down there, I could hear his fleshy lip strings slapping wetly against his chin. "I haven't seen him since the night we burned down the saloon. He's been down here a few times to visit his pets, but, well, there's an awful lot of places to hide."

A few rasping breaths, then he went on. "When I ran off, I came straight here, let myself in the back of the Scarlet Revolver. It was my luck to arrive at such an hour that the halls and bar were deserted. As you know, I kept a room there for years, a sanctuary. Only when I let myself in, did I realize that would be the first place you would look for me. A foolish decision on my part. I tore a sheet from the bed to sop up the blood and recalled the cellar. There were whispered complaints about the smell arising from it, none ever directed to Alexander. As such, the staff ceased keeping anything of worth down there, refrained from visiting the room at all. It would make a good hiding place to nurse my wounds. For a time."

"You saw the light," I said.

I heard him smile again. "So to speak."

"And he just leaves the lantern lit all the time?"

Harvey's face soured, more so. "I tried putting it out, thinking it would draw attention to my presence down here. The animals became … restless."

"I can imagine," I said, rubbing the back of my head. I'd be stiff and sore tomorrow, but with any luck, my mind wouldn't betray me today.

"But once I discovered the treasures within? I knew I had the tools to pay you back. You say my brother didn't die at your hand? Well, I guess there's a little poetry to the whole thing. Nor would you or the girl have died at my hand, if you weren't so stubborn."

"And is our rendezvous just luck, or did you know I was here?"

"Not for sure, but I knew you'd come eventually. And when I heard the explosions … That's just your style, Daggett."

I started to laugh, then it caught in my throat. "Hold on," I said. "If you didn't know all this was down here until after the saloon fire, what about that chimera in the backroom?"

Confusion swirled in his eyes.

"The big fuckin' dragon cat?" I clarified.

The confusion vanished, giving way to amusement in his good eye. There was still a lively quality about it, like that lone eyeball didn't understand how bad the infection was just yet.

"Farrell set it up, didn't he?" I shook the bars, hoping they might give way. Thing was, if they could keep Mogey from getting out, I couldn't offer much of a challenge. "Son of a bitch, you said you didn't see him since that night, but he was the shooter on the roof. Had to have been."

Harvey said nothing.

Slamming a fist against the metal hard enough to split knuckle skin, I shouted, "Talk to me, you fuck!"

"I think I'm all talked out, Daggett. All this time alone down here and I still haven't decided whether I'd like to feed you to those worms—nasty creatures, their saliva dissolves skin, you know—or if I should just put a bullet in your skull and be done with it."

"Do I get a vote?"

He ignored me and went on. "Eventually Locke and the little girl'll come looking for you. That was dumb as hell to leave them, by the way. Noble, just dumb. And when they do, no one'll ever find the bodies." He paused a moment, chest heaving, struggling for breath. He licked his lips and the way his tongue poured out over the missing side of his mouth nearly brought up my supper. "Eventually, it'll be Alexander's turn," he added.

I closed my eyes and let the anger drain away, loosened my grip on the bars. "You ain't wrong, Harvey. It was awful fuckin' dumb of me to let you sneak up on me, but truly, I resent the fact that you think I'd be stupid enough to leave Alice out of all the fun."

That swirl of confusion returned to Harvey's good eye, then shot to fear almost as quickly when he heard the *click* of Alice cocking her revolver. Her color didn't look much better, still grayer than grave dirt. Whatever effects of her vision lingered, her eyes had cleared, and her shooting hand was steady.

"Thick as thieves, you two," he muttered, holding up his empty hands. "Should've guessed the mongrel wouldn't be far behind the bitch." Harvey watched me with the same animal look as most of the things in cages and spat. "You see my face, Daggett? What your sheriff did to me? It burns something fierce, aches all the time. My forehead's on fire and I'm drenched in sweat, even when I feel cold. Maybe that bullet's still in there, maybe it's lying in a ditch somewhere. Point is, I'm likely done for. I know that. My only hope was that you'd get down here in time and I could take you with me." Sweat dripped down his face and the rotting smell grew stronger, as if to prove his point. "What are you waiting for then, girl? Do it!" he barked.

From around his side, Alice dropped her free hand and rubbed her pointer finger and thumb together twice.

"What do I do?" she was asking.

I gripped the bars again, squeezed, and tried not to show anything on my face. If I still had my revolver, I might've shot Harvey myself. Sure, he might be dead in a few days when the poison in his head found its way to the rest of his body, but in the meantime, how many more people would I let him kill?

And here I was, a weapon in the form of a little girl aimed right at his head, and all I had to do to pull the trigger was say a word. Even a head nod would do. The three of us kept that stand-off going for ages, a thousand years if it was a minute.

A sharp notion of right and wrong. The ability to make those decisions on your own.

Hadn't that been what I said?

"Please," said Alice, rubbing a flat palm in a circle around her chest.

I couldn't move, couldn't be the one to point that weapon.

If I thought I'd been aiming you at things and letting you knock 'em dead all this time, that wouldn't make me much of a father.

"Alice," I said, and hoped it was enough.

Without lowering the revolver, she took a step back. Harvey let out another ugly laugh and lowered his hands.

"Don't move, Moses. She ain't going to shoot an unarmed man, but if you do something she doesn't like, she'll make both sides of your head match."

Another laugh, gritty and grating. "She going to lead me upstairs and to the sheriff's office? Wave her hands around and ask me nicely to get in the cell?" He shook his head. "You could let your daddy out, kid. The key is in my vest pocket. Go ahead, just take a step closer and grab it."

I didn't need to tell her that was a stupid idea.

"So, what's it going to be, girlie? Shoot me or take your chances?"

In fact, I'd say it would make me as much a monster as anyone we've stood together against.

"Alice!" Just as helpful as the first time. Wide blue eyes and the revolver starting to tremble, she stepped toward him, curled her finger around the trigger. Before she could make a choice, something burst out of the dark and took Moses Harvey to the ground, filling the tunnel with the same sound as my knuckles slamming into the metal bars.

Alice stumbled backward over her own feet, still clutching the gun, but clearly unsure where to aim it. From the tumble of bodies, Thaddeus Locke stood up, holding the branding iron from the worm cage. That was the sound. Metal bar meets skull. So you can guess how surprised I was when Moses Harvey clambered to his feet and threw a locomotive-sized punch at Locke.

Walk down. Hazel had seen Alice give those signs the night the Mogollon monster attacked. Then, *animal eyes.* Both had brought us to this place, this time.

Thad ducked the punch and drove the poker into Harvey's stomach, drawing out a sound from the bigger man like a sack of grain splitting. A couple of cracked ribs, at the very least. Still, it didn't slow him down. He wrapped his arms around Thad in a bear hug and squeezed, making Thad drop the iron. *Clank* against the packed dirt. If Harvey could do all this with infection set in, imagine what a healthy version of him would be capable of. Thad kicked his legs, desperately trying to free himself. Harvey held tight. When Thad's legs went still, I thought it might be over, then Thad lifted his head and slammed it forward into the center of Harvey's face. If you stepped on a cougar's tail, it wouldn't have let out such a scream.

Harvey loosened his grip enough for Locke to slip out and fire off a couple lightning-strike punches, one to the face and one to those maimed ribs. The third punch came, and Harvey blocked it with a meaty forearm and grabbed Thad around the neck.

Choke. The last sign, accompanied by Alice's frightened face as she'd held both hands up to her throat. She was making the same face now, frozen in fear.

I dropped to my knees and reached out of the cage for my revolver. Almost. I shoved my arm out as far as it would go. Cold metal bit into my shoulder, and I only succeeded in brushing the gun with my fingertips.

Locke started to purple as Harvey lifted his elbows and squeezed.

"If I only get to take one of you with me," said Harvey, "I'm glad it was you, you bastard."

Locke slapped at Harvey's tree-trunk arms, kicked fruitlessly at his legs. *Someone's going to die tonight.*

Dark as a bruised plum, Thad fought and fought. My fingers stretched for the revolver as I shouted nonsense. Cuts opened on my shoulder as the bars adjusted the shape of my body. Blood dribbled down my arm. Almost, almost.

Harvey squeezed. "I never had need to tell you this before, but me and Farrell? We know about Tuscaloosa. We know about Cambridge. And I bet there's loads more to tell. Shame you won't get the chance."

Locke's eyes went wide enough to catch rain. With a strained effort, he swung both legs back and drove his knees into Harvey's ribs. It was enough. Once again, he squirmed free, fell to the ground, and scrambled for the iron.

Just as I knocked the gun a hair closer and wrapped my fingers around it, Thad wound up a mighty swing and connected with the disfigured side of Harvey's head. The former mayor dropped like a sack of horse shit.

I climbed to my feet, holding my shoulder, revolver dangling from my blood-soaked hand.

"He ain't getting up from that," I said. "Not anytime soon. He still breathing?"

Locke nodded, staring down at Harvey.

Recovered from her stupor, Alice crawled forward and snatched a key from Harvey's vest pocket, then darted over to me and handed it through the bars. Her body was shaking too badly to undo the lock herself. Holding the key, I said, "You thought about how we get the big fucker up topside?"

For a moment, I figured he hadn't heard me. No answer, no movement. Finally, he said, "We don't." Then he looked at me with empty eyes. Killer's eyes. When he spoke again, his voice contained less than his gaze. "I'm sorry about this, Rory. Alice, you should look away."

"Thad?"

He took a deep breath, then kicked Harvey's body onto its back. Moses's eyelids fluttered, and he looked up, seeming to search his surroundings before Thad knelt and jammed the branding iron into his mouth. The metal stifled Harvey's screams but failed to dull the sound of his agony. That choking sound that came from him laughing; it was like that, only worse. A last gasp instead of a warning of things to come.

"What the fuck are you doing?" I fought the key into the lock with blood-slicked hands, dropped it, then snatched it up and tried again. Alice ran to him and smacked him on the back, the arms, pleading for him to stop.

Thad pushed her away, knocking her on her backside. Hurt collected in her eyes.

Deeper and deeper, he shoved the iron down Harvey's throat. The man's legs kicked, either in an attempt to fight or involuntary death throes. It was hard to tell which. His good eye widened, bugging out of his head, threatening to burst. Still, Thad jammed the pole down further. A fleshy squelch, louder than the screams, echoed through the underground chamber. Harvey kicked one last time, then went still just as I managed the door open.

Alice lay on the ground, shock written across her features, and Thad stared at me. I searched for my friend and found no trace of him.

"He would have killed us all," he said.

I searched for an argument and came up empty. All I could do was turn away and help Alice to her feet. Without another word, I tossed the key behind me and set out toward the surface with my little girl, before I could see Moses Harvey's ghost watching me, judging me for failing to put a bullet in my friend and stop the barbarity in his final moments.

Out on the street, we met Nola and Hazel. A nervous excitement colored their every movement.

Hazel wrapped me in a hug that I tried my best to return. "Rory! You were in there so long, I have to admit I was starting to get rattled." Her eyebrows shot up as she stepped back, taking in the sorry sight of me. "Are you okay? You've got a lot of blood on you."

"I'll be alright," I said. "Scraped myself up a fair bit. Nothing mortal."

"We saw Mr. Locke run into the building like his ass was on fire," said Nola. The questions were evident.

What happened? Is he okay?

"Not Farrell," I said, my mouth drier than the outside of a cactus.

Alice set to spelling. Hazel watched each letter with care.

"Harvey?" she asked. "Mayor Harvey? What—"

"He's dead," I put in. "Harvey is. I guess that's all that matters."

"Where is Thad?" asked Nola, staring over my shoulder. My heart jumped, worried he might appear, and I'd have to figure out what to say to him.

"Wrapping up something. I expect he'll be along any time." I started to walk away.

"Did Locke save you all?" asked Hazel and brought me to a quick stop.

Don't you lie to her, Daggett.

I checked with Alice and saw no help in her eyes. Giving her a look that I hoped collected all my scattered thoughts, I said, "I guess he did."

It wasn't a lie, not really. Without Locke's intervention, I'd still be trapped in Mogey's cage, Alice locked in a standoff with Harvey. Still, neglecting to mention that I'd stood by, revolver in hand, while Thad brutally murdered Harvey, it didn't quite feel the same as leaving out the bloody details about the Noose story. I guess tomorrow I'd just have to be a better man.

"Thank you for all your help, Miss Kane, Miss Betts. For everything, truly. I'm sorry, I … I guess we better get on home. I'm awfully tired."

Nola took a step back, not bothering to hide the confusion written across her face. She deserved an explanation every bit as much as Hazel. One that damned me, Locke, or the both of us equally. "Alright," she said.

Hazel stayed quiet. As Alice and I started toward the town's southwest line, I caught a look in Hazel's eye. This time I was sure it was disappointment.

Chapter 23

Inside the Gray

"Get your filthy boots off my desk, Daggett."

Any trace of the jovial version of Alexander Farrell that stood in front of a crowd and stirred them into a frenzy had faded away when he shut the door to his office. Before me sat a man who was cold and cagey and didn't give much of a fuck that you saw either one. A man who figured I wouldn't pull my revolver and put one between his eyes with the same kind of certainty that told most people water would quench your thirst.

Slowly, I met his request and lowered my legs, not bothering to wipe away the bits of dirt I'd left in my wake.

Farrell pinched the bridge of his nose. "I'm a busy man, Daggett. Got a town to run, as you well know. All the same, you have added another name to your long list of rogues who won't plague the town of Buzzard's Edge again. In total, Moses Harvey is responsible for the deaths of ..." He shuffled through his stack of papers and pretended to study one, like he didn't have the figure in his head already. "Five citizens, that we know of."

"And a horse."

He held out a hand to concede the point. "So, I suppose I owe you an audience."

"Mighty big of you, Alex."

"Why are you here?" Hands folded, eyes squinting.

I clucked my tongue. "Truth?"

"Are we not both men of truth?"

"That's the thing. I don't know what kind of man you are. I've got an idea, sure, and I've heard some stories. Hoo boy, if half of 'em are true, I oughta drag you down the stairs right this minute and shoot you in the street."

As I sat across from Farrell, I remembered my promise to Vivian and Drea.

What if we could stop it from happening again?

Farrell tented his fingers and let the hint of a smirk onto his face. "Ah, but there's the problem with being the hero of Buzzard's Edge. Such behavior would be unbecoming."

"I've been thinking about that, actually. That's not a name I ever asked for. Not one I particularly care for, either. All I ever did was what felt right at the time. Sometimes that's protecting somebody who can't protect themselves, sometimes it's chasing down a killer, so they won't do it again. I wouldn't call myself a vengeful person, but I can see how the term might stick."

That smirk stayed on his face, but there wasn't any humor left in it. "Do you have a point?" he asked.

"Only that with the election behind us, Mr. Mayor, one of the people in this room is duty bound to do right by the people of Buzzard's Edge, and after the last fella that held the office? People'll be watching very, very closely. Hell, I plan to be one of them. Now, the other person in this room? He doesn't have to impress a soul."

"That person seems to be forgetting their ties to the sheriff's office."

Those ties were loose, at best, and Farrell knew it. What I hoped he didn't know was how much they'd frayed around the edges lately.

"If you made the argument that I've got stock in some people in this town, you'd be dead on. In fact, most folks trying to protect their daughters would worry about marching up those stairs to tell the man who runs the town to get his shit together if he wants to keep his head on his shoulders."

"Don't forget about that pretty little schoolteacher."

My stomach dropped like a stone. It'd been days since I talked to Hazel, promising myself I'd find the words before I tried. Lo and behold, they'd evaded me. The disconnect was all in my head. If I let enough time pass before being honest with her, completely honest, well, she might not want to talk to me anymore, and I didn't think I could bear that. Thinking of holding her hand under the warm sun and the way Alice had come around to her … Maybe I had more than one person worth fighting for after all.

"Then again," I said, "most folks probably aren't aware of your underground circus. I expect it'll be easy enough to put all the blame on Harvey; even pretend you had no idea that all those critters were down there. And the people of Buzzard's Edge will eat it up because they don't know what's in that bottom drawer there." I let my eyes track down, then swept them back up to see the momentary panic on his face. "Right on top of a pistol. You could go for it, but I'd bet all the quills on a cactus cat I could beat you to the draw."

Farrell held still, waiting. The panic fell from his face and his new, flat expression gave nothing away.

"You asked me to get to the point, Farrell. I know you helped Harvey burn down the saloon, probably execute the two people inside as well. For damn sure, I know you helped him get that chimera in there, not that I can guess at how you got something that big, sharp, and mostly on fire across town." I raised an eyebrow, hoping he might let me in on the secret. No such luck. "I know you took those shots from the rooftop, got me in the leg, and would've killed both me and Locke if you had better aim. I won't go so far as 'know' but I suspect you fixed the election somehow, if only because it certainly seems up your alley given all the other shit. And I know if I laid out proof of all that, the people would drag you through the streets and hang you high."

"Is it so hard to believe the townspeople put their faith in me?" He rested his hand on the bottom drawer, and I suspect he didn't even know he was doing it. "Besides, you have no proof ... of any of these wild allegations."

"Well now, Alex, here's where we come back to the part about you needing public approval and me, not so much. Doesn't fucking matter if I can prove it. I just want it to stop. And that includes those stories I hear about girls going missing from your brothel here once they've worn out their welcome."

His eyes narrowed and made me real glad I'd opted not to mention anyone by name.

"If it does stop," I went on, "maybe you and I, we can learn to tolerate each other. If not, then good news. I won't need anybody's permission to kill you."

He sat stone-faced, then let a snicker escape. "You say you wouldn't call yourself vengeful, even after you tracked down and murdered an entire gang. Yet you would accuse me of all these terrible things and let me off with a stern warning? Perhaps Rory Daggett is growing up, seeing his place in the world, and understanding the way of things. Not all is black and white, young man. Even one such as you can learn to live inside the gray."

"I can think of at least a dozen folks I'd prefer to have a philosophical discussion on morals and ethics with over you, Alex. So, here's what we're going to do. First and foremost, it's godawful you got all these animals stuck in holes below ground for your personal pleasure. You're going to let them go. And," I said, raising my index finger, "for the love of all things, assuming you've got some back ways out of that underground purgatory, get it done far away from here, so we don't lose anymore folks to animal attacks. I'll be checking in to see that you go through with it, and lordy, by this point, I hope you know I can do it."

I'd seen anger on Farrell's face, fear, arrogance, and a host of other blink-and-you-miss-it expressions. Never sadness, though. Not until that moment. His face fell and his eyes glistened. "I've collected these creatures for years. Some I've raised from birth. They are my pets." He stopped short of saying he loved them, but only just. He looked down as if an argument might be scrawled across his desk, and a strange thought crossed my mind. What if it was shooting Ghost that made Farrell abandon Moses Harvey?

A dozen responses ran through my head, most having to do with kicking the man when he was down. I settled on saying, "You know it's the right thing and they'll be better off."

When he looked back up, there was a flash of anger, followed by acceptance. He gave a quick nod, and that was good enough for me. I shifted in my seat, planning a request and hoping I didn't have to turn it into a demand.

"I'll be straight, Alex. I don't really trust you, but I'm hopeful. Hopeful that a fair portion of all the shit stewing out under the sun lately was on Harvey. That you're just a greedy prick with a temper, because those things can be controlled. I'm asking you, do this thing right. You make it clear you can take care of the people here, and you and I, we won't have a problem. Otherwise?" I shrugged, then stood up to leave.

What if we could stop it from happening again?

Maybe, just maybe, fixing things didn't always need to end in death.

"Daggett," he said, as I reached the door.

Hand on the familiar handle, I turned. His pistol sat on his desk. I saw it and he knew I saw it, but he kept his eyes on me. There was something shrewd in there, and not something I altogether cared for. Could a man change? Sure, but I didn't have high hopes this would be the last time I had to threaten Alexander Farrell.

"We buried Moses Harvey, privately, next to his brother. Did you know that?"

"I heard. Didn't think it was appropriate for me to attend."

He nodded. "His corpse. It was mutilated."

I winced, couldn't hold it back.

The small grin he put on said he'd seen it. "Yeah, I didn't figure you did that. That doesn't seem you." He stroked his short-cropped beard and lost himself in thought for a moment. "You've asked an awful lot of favors from me today, and I'd say I've been accommodating. Do you agree?"

"More or less."

"Do one for me." He gave me no time to respond. "Just think about something for me. You don't need to answer. We don't even need to ever talk about it again." He folded his hands in front of him. "How did Mr. Locke know to find you down in the underground tunnel?"

The words hung in the air, and though he'd told me I didn't need to answer, I bet we both knew why I held my tongue.

"You have a good day, Rory Daggett. Mind you shut the door on your way out."

On the way down the stairs, I hadn't bothered making eye contact with Big Lou, any of the regulars, or Mr. Pink out front. I'm sure there were mean faces and muttered curses. Let 'em. Fine by me. With any luck, I'd never have to step foot in that hellhole again.

As I left the Scarlet Revolver in the dust, Alice fell in stride beside me. I kept a close watch on her, waited for the questions to come, except they never did. Sooner or later, we'd have to check in with Nola Betts. She deserved to be kept apprised, after all. I wondered how happy she'd be that I let Farrell off the hook with a wrist slap. Hazel Kane was a tougher one, for a bunch of reasons. Maybe I'd bite that bullet tomorrow.

Another glance at Alice, walking tall and with this easy confidence in her gait. Goddammit, she looked older. Went by Allie with a select few. Not that long now and she'd be ten years old, which was miles from nine in a way that defied description. If she wanted to learn how to sew up clothes at Nola's shop, I'd have to let her. If she wanted to go to school, I couldn't stop her. Even if it meant hearing other kids call her Allie, if it meant putting a good scare into the boys that came courting. She'd always be Alice to me, always Pip.

It drew a smile on my face. She noticed, but didn't ask about that either. In that moment, I was glad Farrell had taken the election. I was glad I had no official ties to the sheriff's office, though I'd be lying if I said my stomach wasn't still sour thinking about Thad Locke.

There was a certain sense of responsibility to Buzzard's Edge, for sure, a desire to keep things from devolving into blood and chaos. I didn't have to ask Alice; I knew her heart. Our main responsibility, as ever, was to each other. Just a couple of song dogs, a little closer to human than people wanted to give us credit for.

Afterword

I've said it before and I'll say it again, I would write these characters and this town until the sun burns out. Watching Rory and Alice grow—and it is watching, dear reader, I have no more control over what they do than you—from strangers to family to father/daughter; it warms my heart, entertains me endlessly, and feels like being with friends. I do apologize for Ghost's untimely demise, and I assure you, that was the hardest death I've written in this series to date. Yeah, I hate me too.

In a way, this book is a love letter to cryptids, ranging from mythological beasts (which, let's face it, are just historical cryptids) like the chimera to more modern fare, like the chupacabra. Through writing this book, I discovered that chupacabras have only held that name since about 1995. Still, I figured most of our myths have been around longer than the names we give them. The Mogollon (moh-ghee-yon) monster is the southwest's own Bigfoot legend, and the story that Henry told Rory is my variation on a real legend surrounding it, although naming the man Gideon was my addition. The stabby bird that attacks off page is called a snallygaster, a particularly nasty piece of work. Underground, we see the Thunderbird, Flatwoods Monster, a Cactus Cat, and Mongolian Death Worms. All based on real cryptids, or at least real stories of things people have seen. What can I say? I want to believe. Of course, if you keep your eyes peeled, you also might recognize the giant Gila monster from "Salvia Sunset" in *Where the Daybreak Ends*.

There will be more Buzzard's Edge stories to come. When and what shape they'll take, I can't say for sure, but I love this place too much to leave it alone.

A tremendous thank you to Heather and Steve at Brigids Gate Press for bringing the first two books back to life and giving the last two a home. To Val Halvorson, for his amazing cover work. Val never fails to capture the essence of these stories. Anyone else's work on the trade covers would feel wrong.

To Candace Nola, for her sharp edits and understanding of Rory's voice, as well as for lending her name to a character who I don't think we've seen the last of. To Tyler Jones, for his wonderful stories and wonderful lies, because otherwise I wouldn't have been convinced I could write this book. To Drew Huff, for the conversations and the semblance of sanity. And, of course, to Aron and the boys for granting me the time and grace to disappear to 19th century Arizona for long periods of time. I love you all, unconditionally.

Lastly, to all the readers, reviewers, and booksellers who have taken a chance on these books, western fans or decidedly not, and found something to love in these people and their stories.

LAGNIAPPE

During a staff meeting one gloriously stormy night, the idea of having a "Lagniappe" near the end of some of the works published by Brigids Gate Press was discussed. The staff unanimously voted in favor of the idea.

Lagniappe (pronounced LAN-yap) is an old New Orleans tradition where merchants give a little something extra along with every purchase. It's a way of expressing thanks and appreciation to customers.

The Lagniappe section might contain a short story, a small handful of poems, or a non-fiction piece.

For the lagniappe for this book, the author decided to throw in an extra story, "Calling to Quiet," for all his readers Hope y'all enjoy it.

Calling to Quiet

A murmur of voices filled the Josiah Dennis Schoolhouse. It's what every morning sounded like before Hazel Kane reached across her desk and gave the small brass bell a single ring to call the class to quiet. Until then, she would sit and listen. It was her favorite time of the day.

"—daddy took me out in the bare desert and let me shoot a couple rounds. The pistol kicked like you wouldn't believe. My arm's still sore!"

"—bought me a dress 'cept I'm not s'posed to wear it to school 'cause I might get it dirty. Just for Sundays, and even then, I gotta change right when I get home."

"—not making it up! I saw it and so did my little brother. Flew across the sun and its wings were as wide as this whole building."

When a small figure filled the open doorway, Hazel started to grab for the bell, then gave it another moment. The girl had warm red cheeks and cold blue eyes, and she looked peculiar without a holster tugging at her hip. Smaller, somehow. She fiddled with her hands as she waited to be noticed and Hazel wondered if she'd set out with the sun, spending a couple hours at Nola's shop before coming this way.

Hazel also couldn't help wondering what the girl's daddy was up to and when she might get to talk to him again about more than a formal enrollment. She smiled at Alice and Alice offered a half-hearted version back, then stood up a little straighter and looked more herself. A quick ring of the bell before Hazel set it down and dampened the sound.

"Good morning, class."

"Good morning, Miss Kane."

"This is our new student, Alice."

Chairs scraped as the class turned to take her in. For a moment, there was nothing but silence. Hazel's throat went dry. Then, just as they'd practiced, all thirteen boys and girls held out their right hands, palms up, let them sit a second, then drew them back toward their stomachs.

"Welcome," they said, though not a word was spoken.

About the Author

Brennan LaFaro is a music teacher by day, horror writer by night, living in southeastern Massachusetts with his wife, two sons, and his hounds. He is the author of the Slattery Falls trilogy, the Buzzard's Edge Saga, as well as Illusions of Isolation and Last Stay. You can read his short fiction in various anthologies and find him at www.brennanlafaro.com.

More from Brigids Gate Press

MELINDA WEST AND THE GREMLIN QUEEN: 2

(MONSTER GUNSLINGERS)

KC Grifant

In an alternate Old West, monsters rule the land—but one deadly duo is humanity's last hope.

Melinda West is a sharpshooter with a steady hand, a cool head and a no-nonsense attitude. Her partner, Lance, brings the charm—and the firepower. Together, they've made a living hunting supernatural threats. But when a strange illness leaves a trail of corpses in its wake, they realize they're about to face their greatest challenge yet.

As the bodies pile up, a swarm of gremlins—smarter, faster and deadlier than anything they've encountered before—are hellbent on destruction. Unless Melinda and Lance can uncover the truth behind these mysterious creatures, everything they know will be torn apart.

Fast-paced, gritty, and packed with supernatural thrills, Melinda West and the Gremlin Queen blends the rebellious charm of Bonnie

and Clyde with the high-stakes action of Supernatural and Buffy the Vampire Slayer.

This is book two in a standalone interconnected series—ideal for both new readers and returning fans looking for dark fantastical westerns with a twist.

BLOOD ON THE SOIL, TERROR ON THE WIND

Ed. Kenneth W. Cain

Whether in an old weathered mine shaft, somewhere off the beaten path, out in the woods, or right here in the middle of this ghost town, danger awaits. We're going to take you way back, drop you right smack dab in the middle of the Old West at its finest. But we're not just going to give you shootouts and bullet wounds and blood splatter. Yes, those things are prominently featured, but there's so much more to this anthology of western horror.

Maybe it's a well-known creature popping in for a visit, or some new creepy crawly monster sucking out your soul, we're going to turn the Old West inside-out and explore its guts to the fullest. There are new adventures to be had, monsters both familiar and unfamiliar to be thwarted… And we're not always going to be the victors. Life in the Old West is hard, trying at its best, and it can wear you down quick.

So, prepare yourself to be transported back in time. Get yourself up on that rickety stagecoach, draw your guns, and let's get going. There's vast territory to cover here, and your journey begins now.

THE SEETHING

Ben Monroe

A family's relocation looked like a chance to relax and regroup—but as they settle into their new home, teenage Kimmie Barnes' special senses make her the target of something primordial, evil, and utterly malign.

Darkness…

Golden Oaks, California is a sleepy town on the shores of Oro Lake, and the residents have no idea what horrors lurk below the glittering waters.

Beneath the waves…

One by one, as people begin to disappear, the once quiet town is soon in the grips of a waking nightmare. An unimaginable horror consuming everything before it.

Hungry…

All while echoes of an ancient evil spread out like malignant spider webs, like dead hands reaching, grasping…

SEETHING…

THE WOODCUTTER

Stephanie Ellis

A tragic accident, shrouded in mystery, leads to a family reunion in the hidden village of Little Hatchet, located in the smothering shadow of GodBeGone Wood, the home of the mythical Woodcutter and Grandma. Alec Eades rediscovers his bond with GodBeGone Wood and the future his father agreed to years ago as nefarious landowner Oliver Hayward schemes to raise money for the village by re-enacting part of the Woodcutter legend. Old wounds are re-opened and ties of blood and friendship are tested to the extreme when the Woodcutter is summoned and Grandma returns.

Visit our website at: www.brigidsgatepress.com